AN OUTLAW

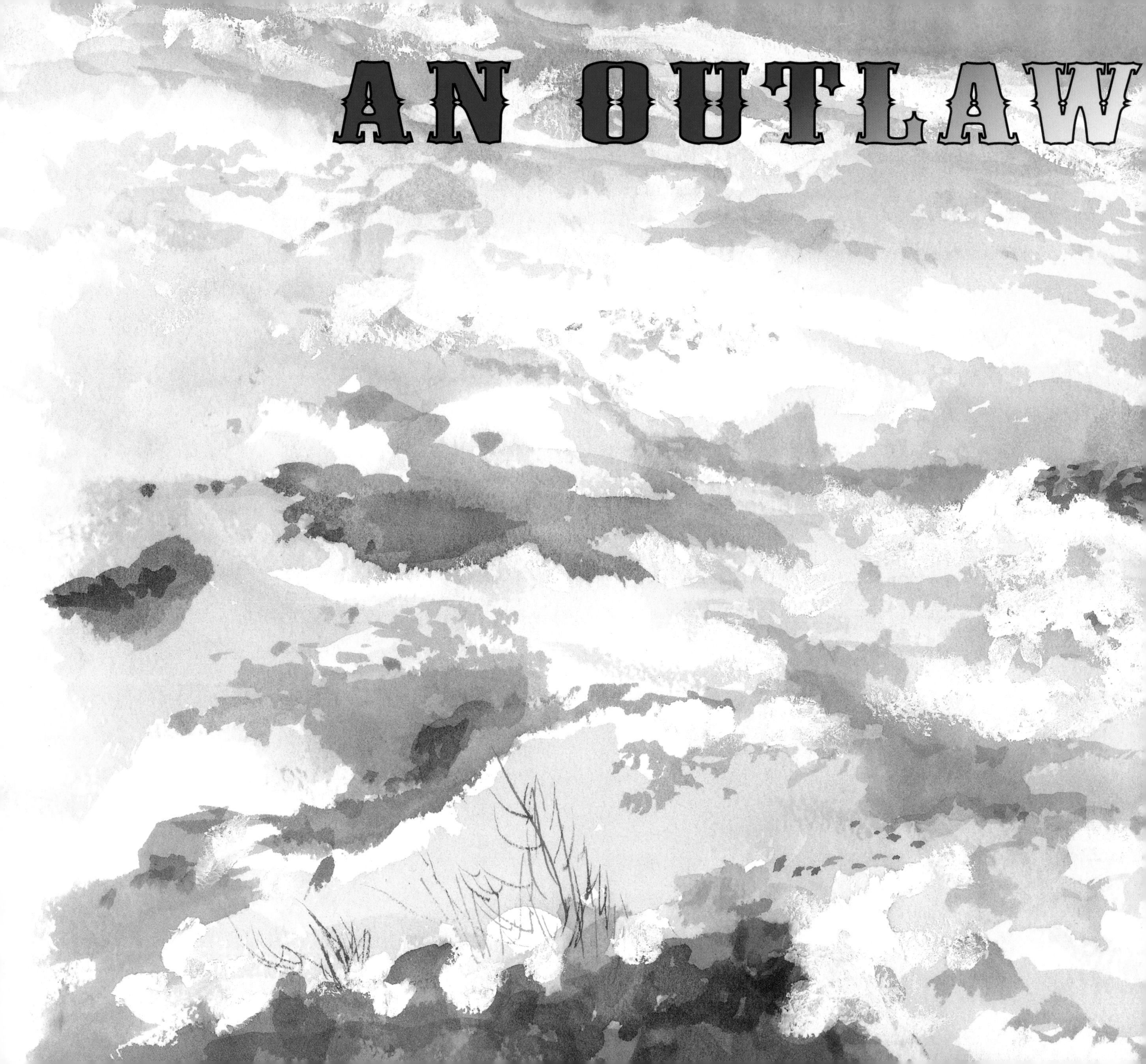

THANKSGIVING

EMILY ARNOLD McCULLY

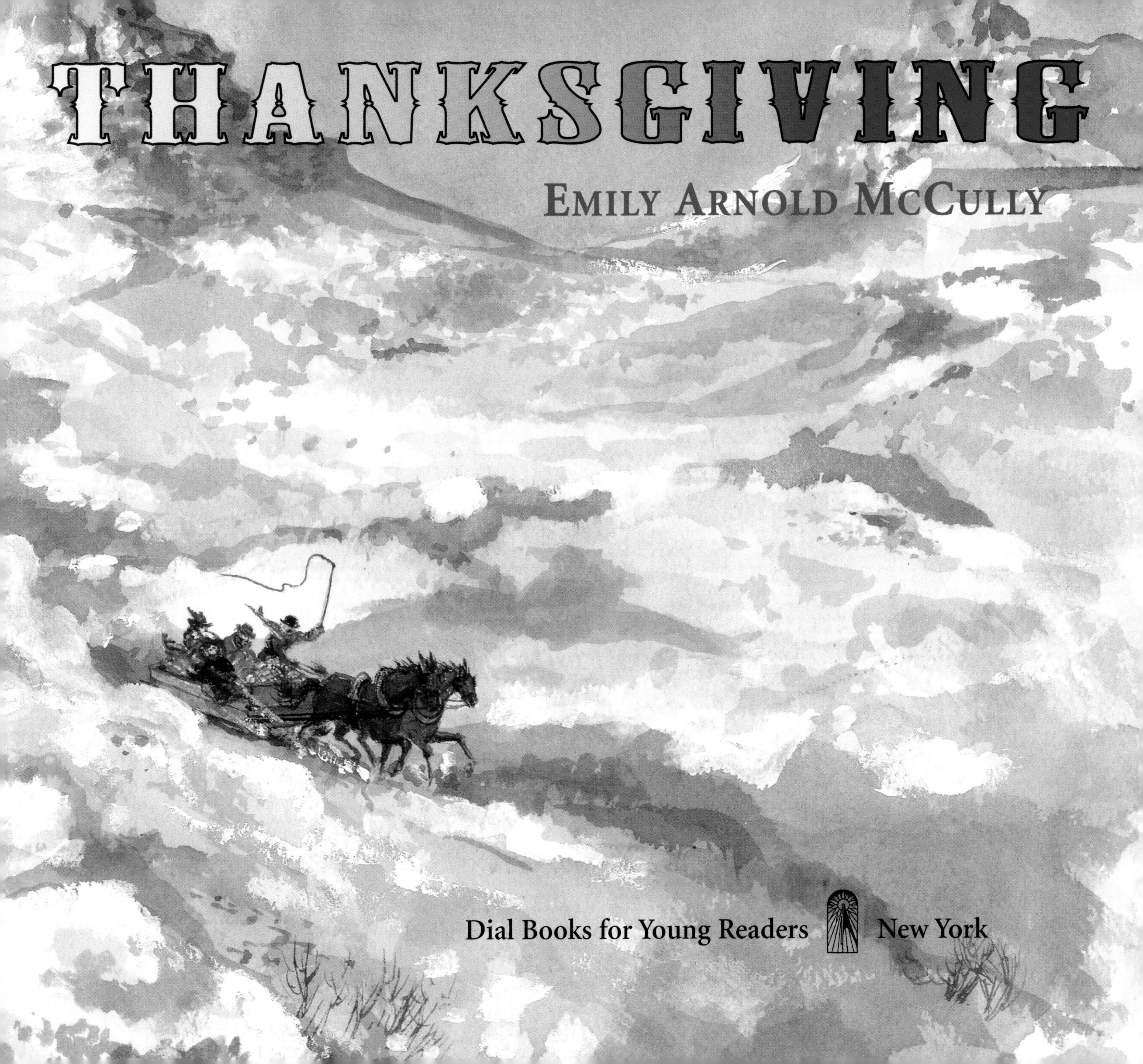

Dial Books for Young Readers New York

Published by Dial Books for Young Readers
A member of Penguin Putnam Inc.
375 Hudson Street • New York, New York 10014

Copyright © 1998 by Emily Arnold McCully
Designed by Atha Tehon
Printed in Hong Kong on acid-free paper
First Edition
1 3 5 7 9 10 8 6 4 2

Library of Congress Cataloging in Publication Data
McCully, Emily Arnold.
An outlaw Thanksgiving/by Emily Arnold McCully.—1st ed.
p.   cm.
Summary: While traveling with her mother cross-country by train in 1896, a young girl unexpectedly
shares Thanksgiving dinner with the notorious outlaw Butch Cassidy.
ISBN 0-8037-2197-8 (trade).—ISBN 0-8037-2198-6 (lib.)
1. Cassidy, Butch, b. 1866—Juvenile fiction. [1. Cassidy, Butch, b. 1866—Fiction. 2. Railroads—West (U.S.)—Fiction.
3. West (U.S.)—Fiction. 4. Robbers and outlaws—Fiction. 5. Thanksgiving Day—Fiction.] I. Title.
PZ7.M47841Ou   1998
[E]—dc21   97-29553   CIP   AC

The artwork was rendered in watercolor and tempera
on watercolor paper with pastel highlights.

In preparing this book, I traveled to Brown's Hole, now called Brown's Park, and visited John Jarvie's store maintained by
the Utah Bureau of Land Management. Among the most helpful reference materials I consulted were the monograph "John
Jarvie of Brown's Park" by William L. Tennent, published in 1981 by the Utah BLM, and *The Bassett Women* by Grace
McClure (Swallow Press/Ohio University Press, 1985). From *The American Heritage History of Railroads in America* by Oliver
Jensen (American Heritage Publishing Co./Bonanza Books, 1981) came valuable railroad information, including the 1893
tourist map of the Union Pacific and connecting lines, on which my map is based. I would like to thank the staff of
the Utah State Historical Society for checking the facts in the book, and Bill Kratville of the Union Pacific Museum in
Omaha, Nebraska, for his help with railroad routes and maps.

FOR PAULA AND MARTIN

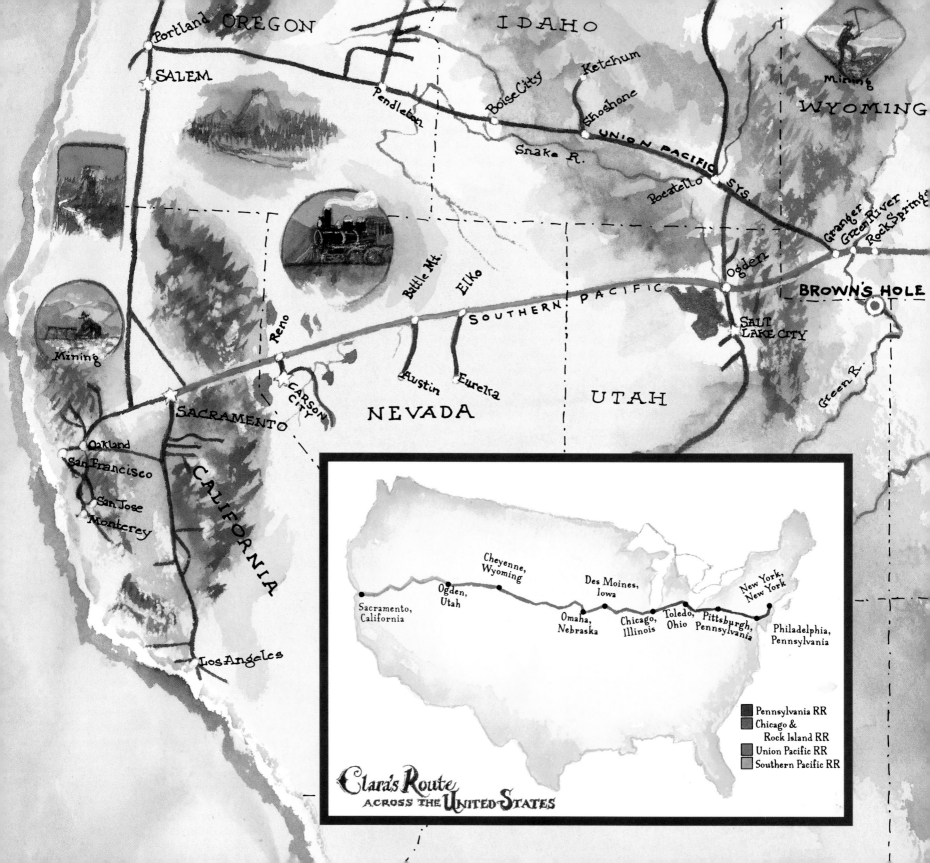

PORTLAND OREGON

SALEM

Pendleton

IDAHO

Boise City

Ketchum

Shoshone

Snake R.

UNION PACIFIC SYS.

Pocatello

WYOMING

Mining

Battle Mt.

Elko

SOUTHERN PACIFIC

Ogden

Granger
Green River
Rock Springs

BROWN'S HOLE

Reno

CARSON CITY

Austin

Eureka

SALT LAKE CITY

Mining

SACRAMENTO

NEVADA

UTAH

Green R.

Oakland
San Francisco
San Jose
Monterey

CALIFORNIA

Los Angeles

Cheyenne,
Wyoming

Ogden,
Utah

Des Moines,
Iowa

New York,
New York

Sacramento,
California

Omaha,
Nebraska

Chicago,
Illinois

Toledo,
Ohio

Pittsburgh,
Pennsylvania

Philadelphia,
Pennsylvania

Pennsylvania RR

Chicago &
Rock Island RR

Union Pacific RR

Southern Pacific RR

Clara's Route
ACROSS THE UNITED STATES

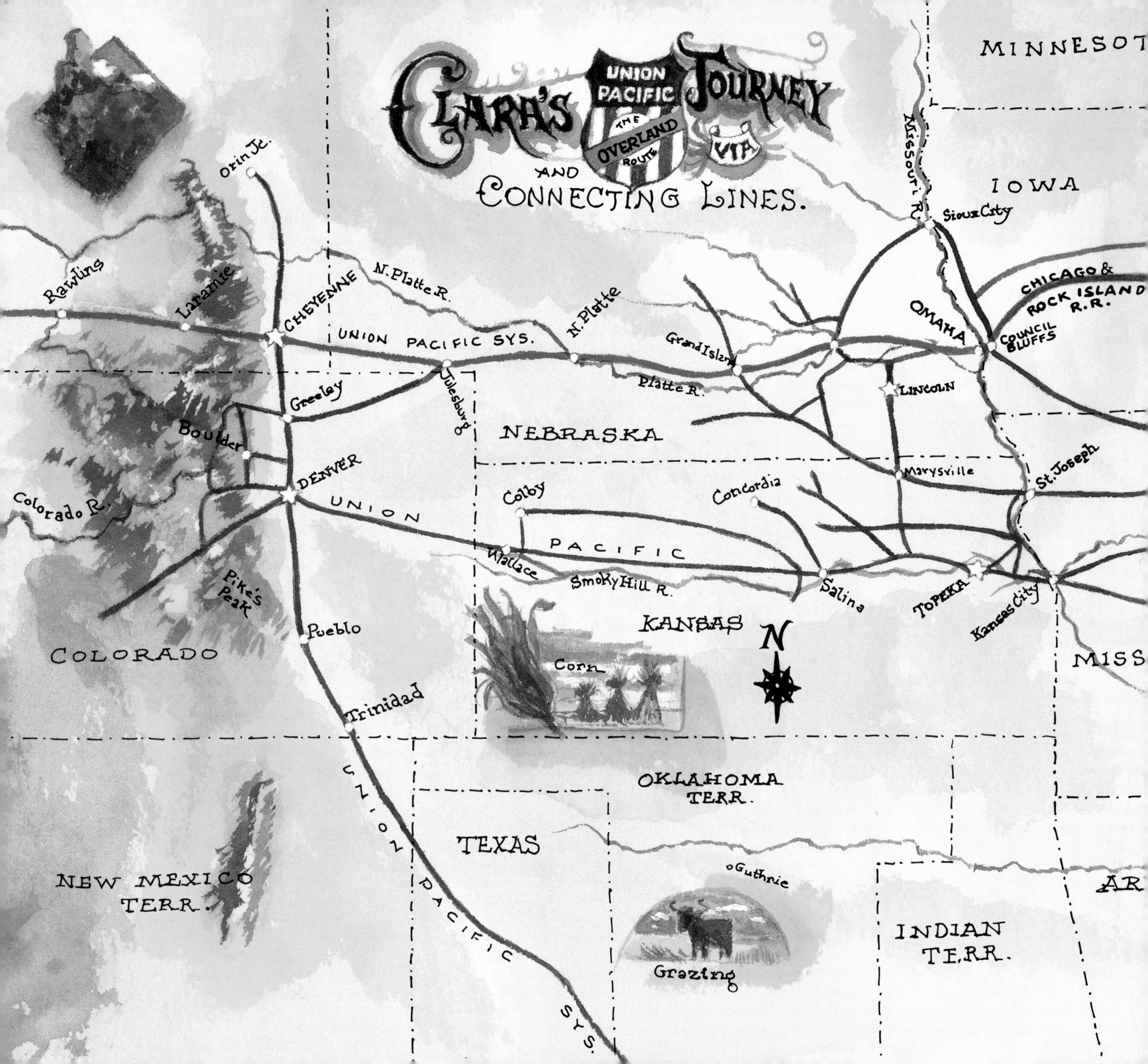
CLARA'S JOURNEY VIA
UNION PACIFIC
THE OVERLAND ROUTE
AND CONNECTING LINES.
MINNESOT
IOWA
Missouri R.
Sioux City
Orin Jc.
Rawlins
Laramie
CHEYENNE
N. Platte R.
UNION PACIFIC SYS.
N. Platte
Grand Island
OMAHA
CHICAGO & ROCK ISLAND R.R.
COUNCIL BLUFFS
Platte R.
LINCOLN
Julesburg
Greeley
Boulder
NEBRASKA
DENVER
Colorado R.
UNION
PACIFIC
Marysville
St. Joseph
Concordia
Colby
Wallace
Smoky Hill R.
Salina
TOPEKA
Kansas City
Pike's Peak
Pueblo
KANSAS
N
COLORADO
Corn
MISS
Trinidad
OKLAHOMA TERR.
UNION PACIFIC SYS.
TEXAS
NEW MEXICO TERR.
oGuthrie
AR
INDIAN TERR.
Grazing

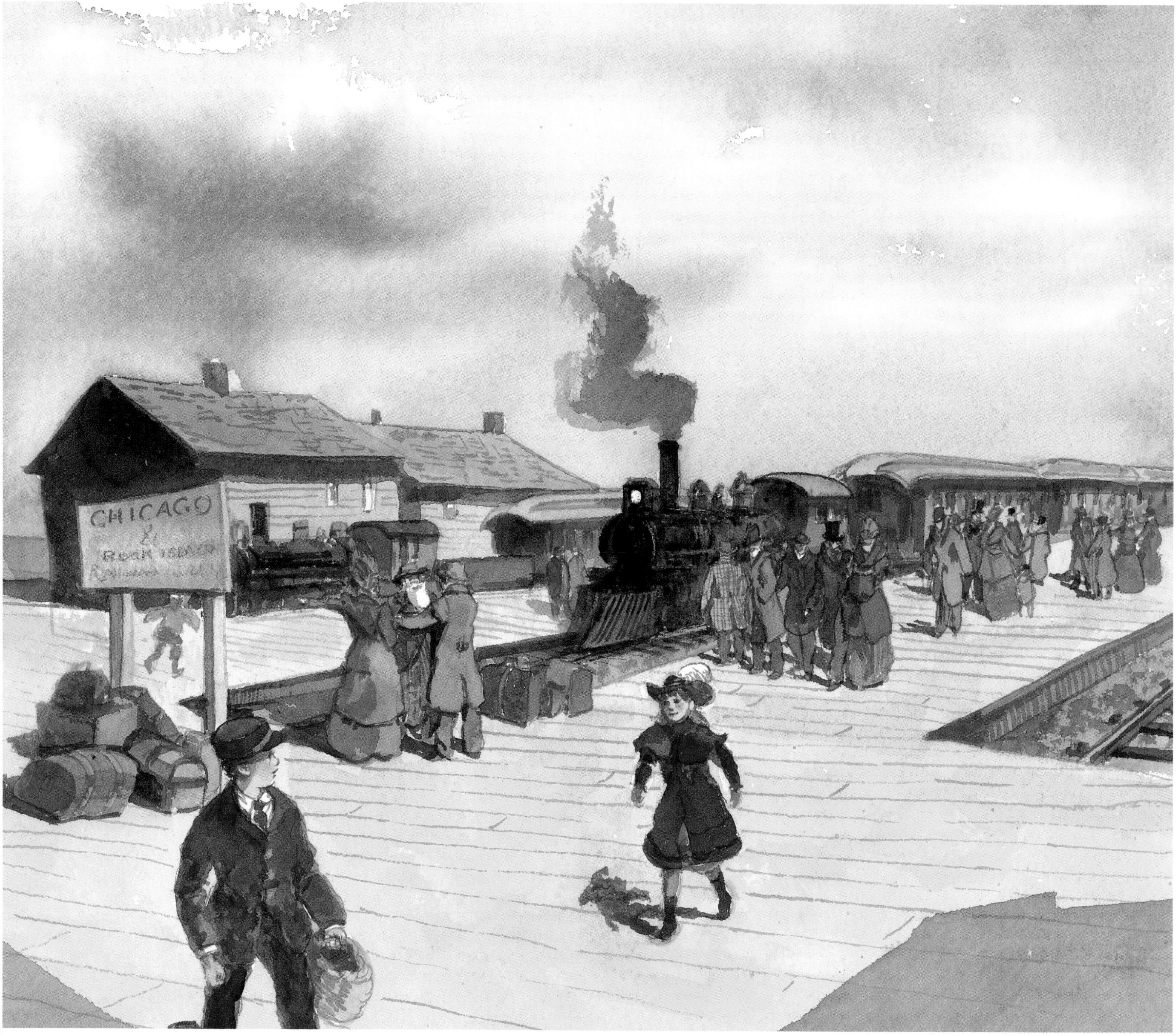
CHICAGO
&

The Chicago and Rock Island Express roared into Omaha, Nebraska, one November day in 1896. Clara Maher was the first one off, eager for a gulp of fresh air after two days in the sooty railcar.

Clara and her mother had come halfway on a journey that had begun in New York State. The day after tomorrow they would meet Papa in Utah and go on to a new life in California.

Her mother hurried into the station to freshen up. Clara set off to explore. "Keep your eyes peeled, coming west," Papa had written. "Out here, you never know what will happen next!"

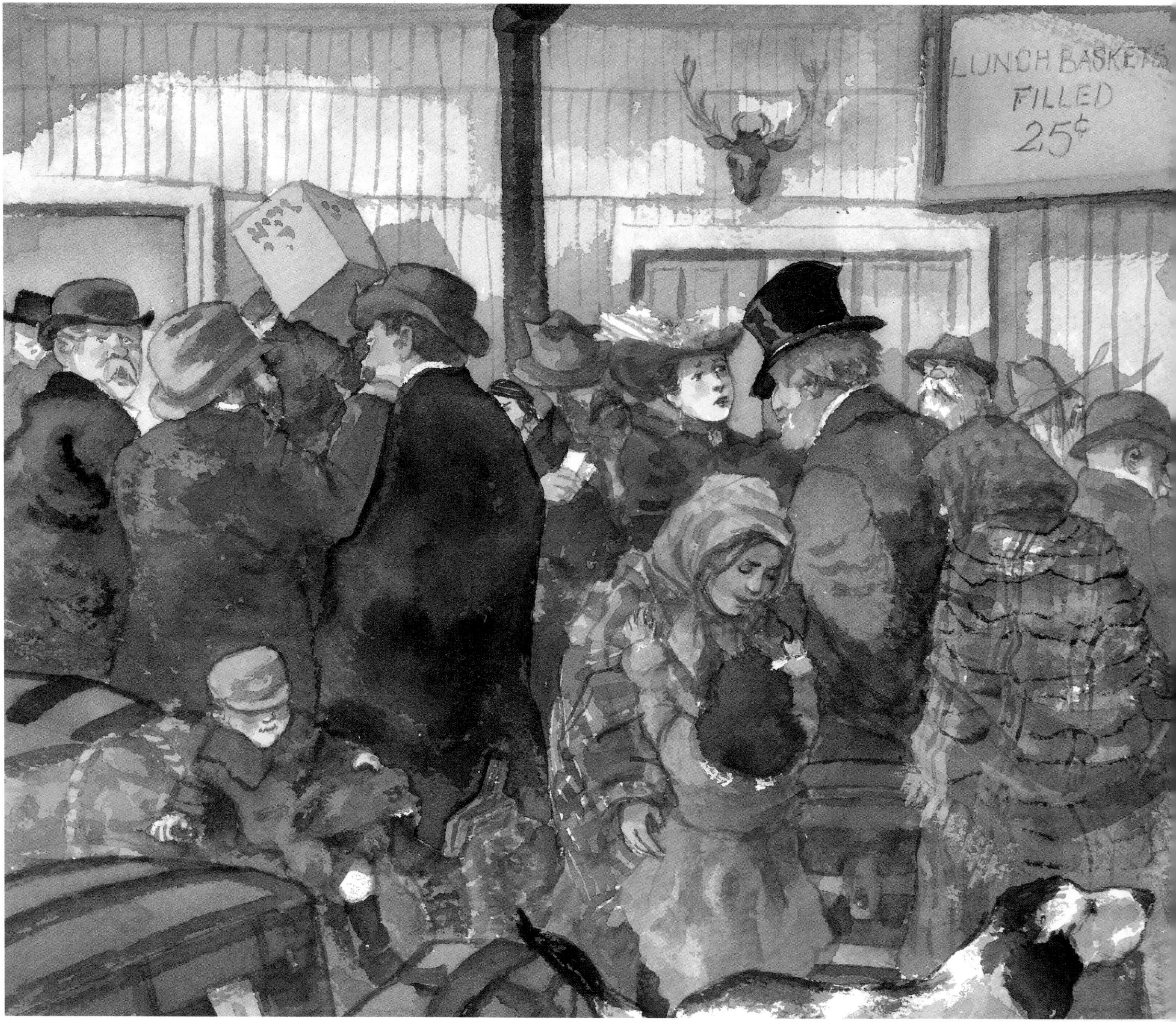
LUNCH BASKETS
FILLED
25¢

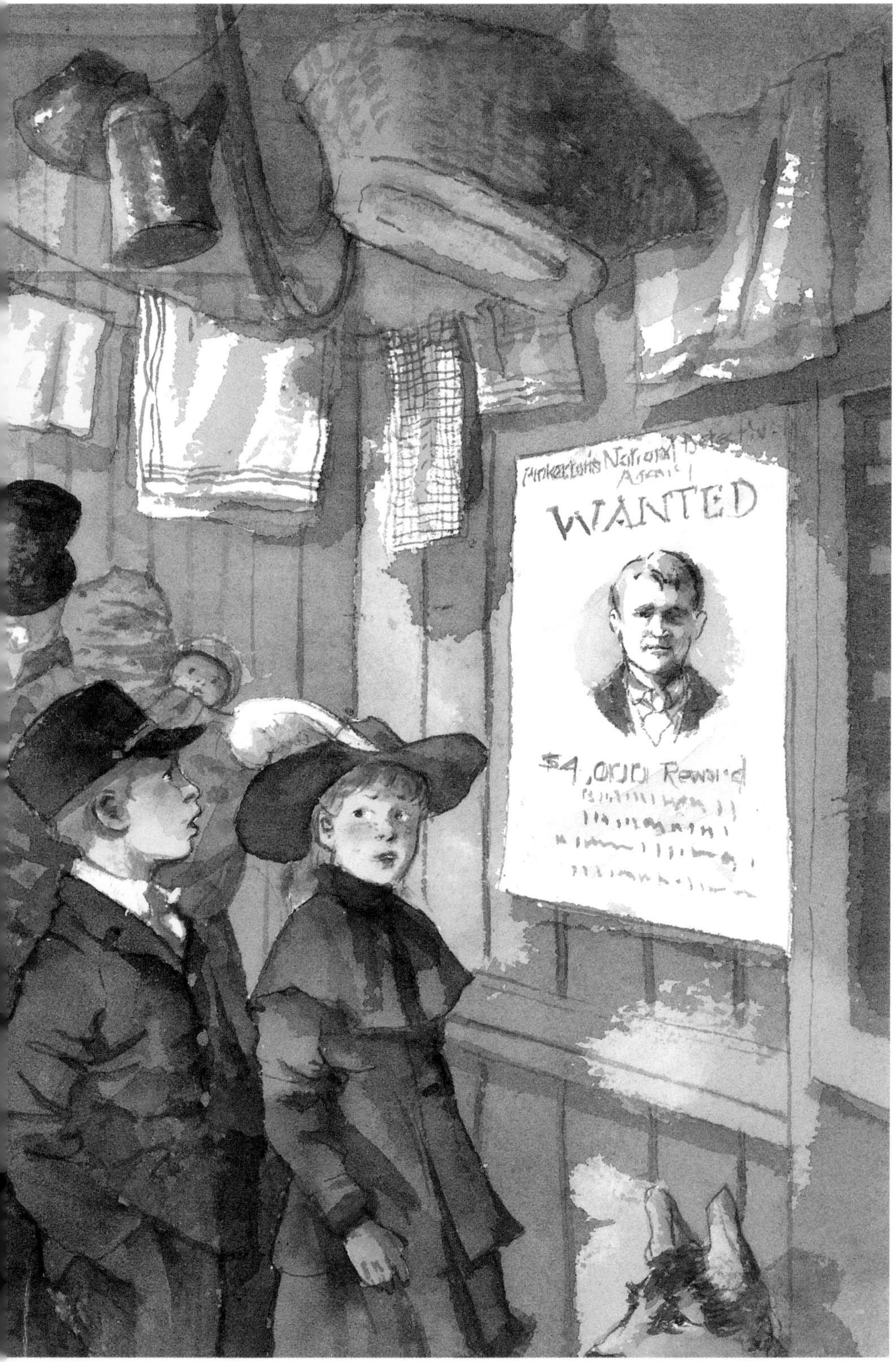
WANTED
$4,000 Reward

She heard a hubbub of strange languages and accents. Emigrants and roughnecks rubbed elbows with travelers in fine clothing. Clara spotted a poster on one wall:

PINKERTON'S NATIONAL
DETECTIVE AGENCY
WANTED
$4,000 Reward
for train robbery, cattle rustling,
bank robbery
Robert LeRoy Parker
alias Butch Cassidy

"I'd sure like to meet him," said a voice. Clara turned in surprise to find the newsboy from the train.

“Butch Cassidy? But he’s an outlaw!” she said.

“No worse than the robber barons who run these railways,” the boy replied with a grin. “Anyway, I think I’d like Butch Cassidy. They say he’s awfully good-hearted. Gives some of what he steals to needy folks. Never killed nobody either.”

“Well, the Pinkertons are after him,” Clara said.

“Butch ain’t afraid of the law or anything else,” the boy said.

Clara wanted to hear more, but Mama had found her. “Clara! You worry me so!” She glanced at the poster and shuddered. “It’s time to transfer to the Union Pacific train,” she went on. “I’ve bought some sandwiches for our supper.”

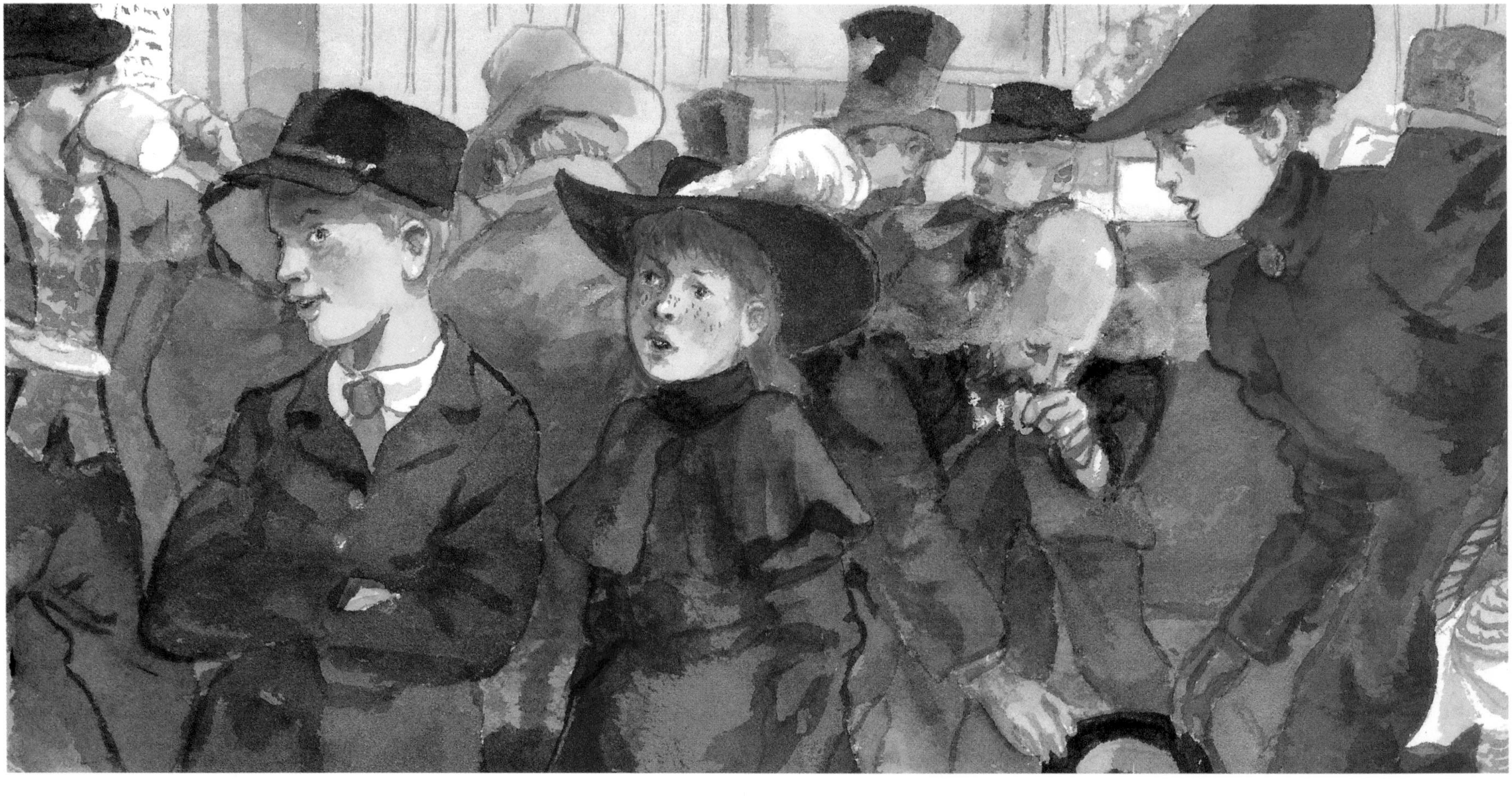

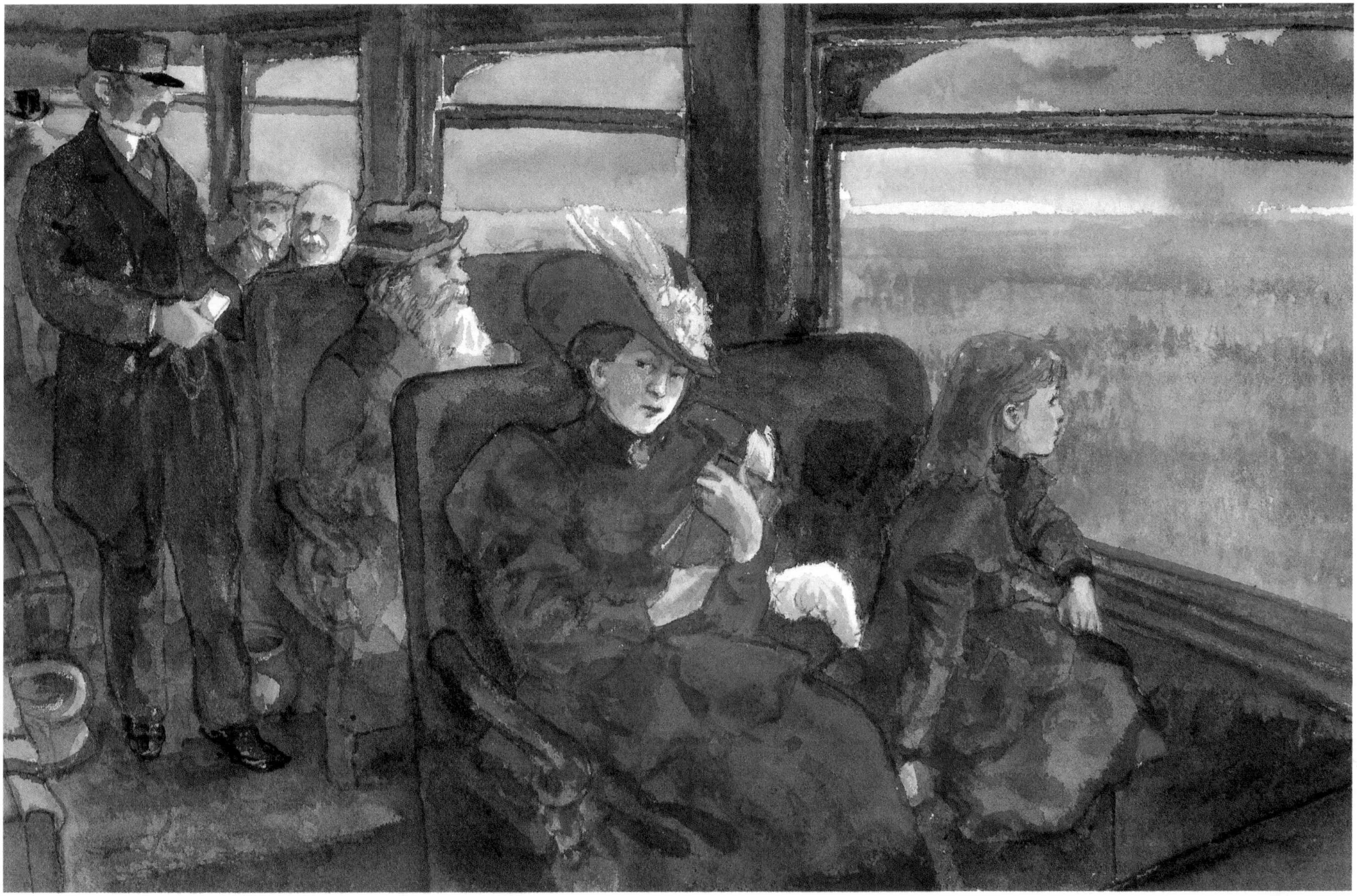

The prairie outside Omaha was as vast as an ocean. Clara stared at it in awe. To stretch her legs, she made her way to the watercooler. Other people drank from the cup the railroad put out, but Mama insisted Clara use the cup she'd brought along. Mama worried about germs, strangers, and train wrecks.

Lamps came on and the sun sank below the endless horizon. People took out their picnic suppers. A few played cards. Clara and Mama wrapped up in their pillows and blankets. They drifted off to sleep to the clackety-clack of the wheels.

In the morning everything was white! Snow fell in thick, churning flakes. "Snowed nearly all night," the conductor said. "We've lost some time." Mama fretted over the news.

Across from them a man was playing a card game. He looked over and said, "Hope they make it up. I've got a big Thanksgiving dinner to get to."

"We'll be with Papa on Thanksgiving Day," said Clara. "We haven't seen him for months. He went to California to start his new business."

The man tipped his hat to Mama. "Clara, we don't know him," her mother whispered. But Clara thought she'd made a friend. He told her his name was Mr. Jones.

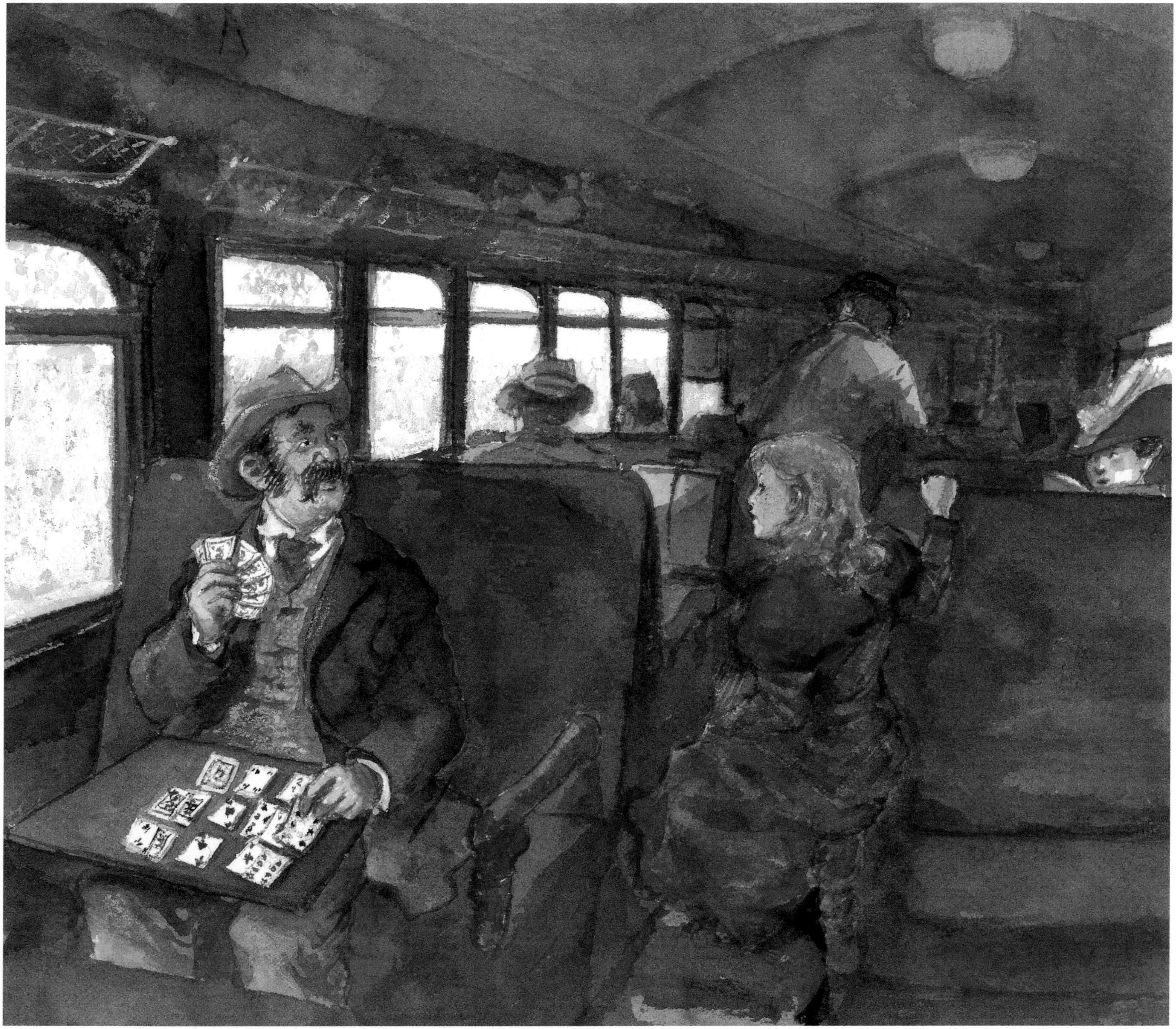

In the afternoon the train lost speed as if exhausted. Finally, with a shudder, it stopped.

The conductor hurried past. "We're snowbound," he announced. "Big drifts blocking us. We'll send for a plow as soon as it stops snowing."

"Mercy!" Clara's mother said. "My husband expects us in Ogden tomorrow."

"You won't make it," said Mr. Jones.

Mama clutched Clara's hand. "Don't worry. Papa will wait for us," Clara assured her.

They sat in the car all day, huddling in their blankets, trying to make their food last. The snow stopped the next morning, but the car was bitterly cold. Through the frosted window, Clara could see mountains ahead.

"We'd better get moving soon," a well-dressed passenger remarked. "If one of those train robbers took a fancy to us, we'd be sitting ducks!" Mama gasped.

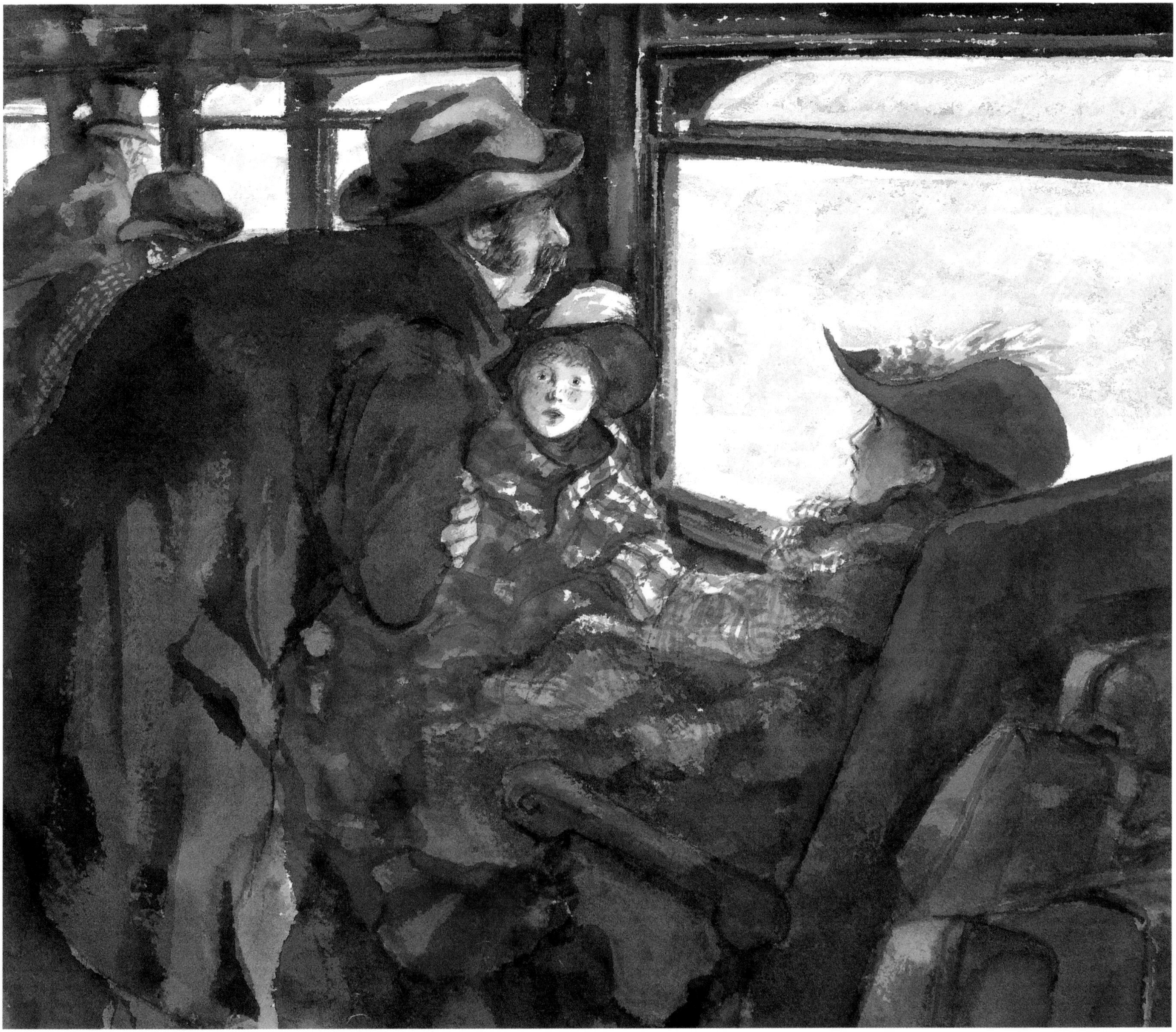

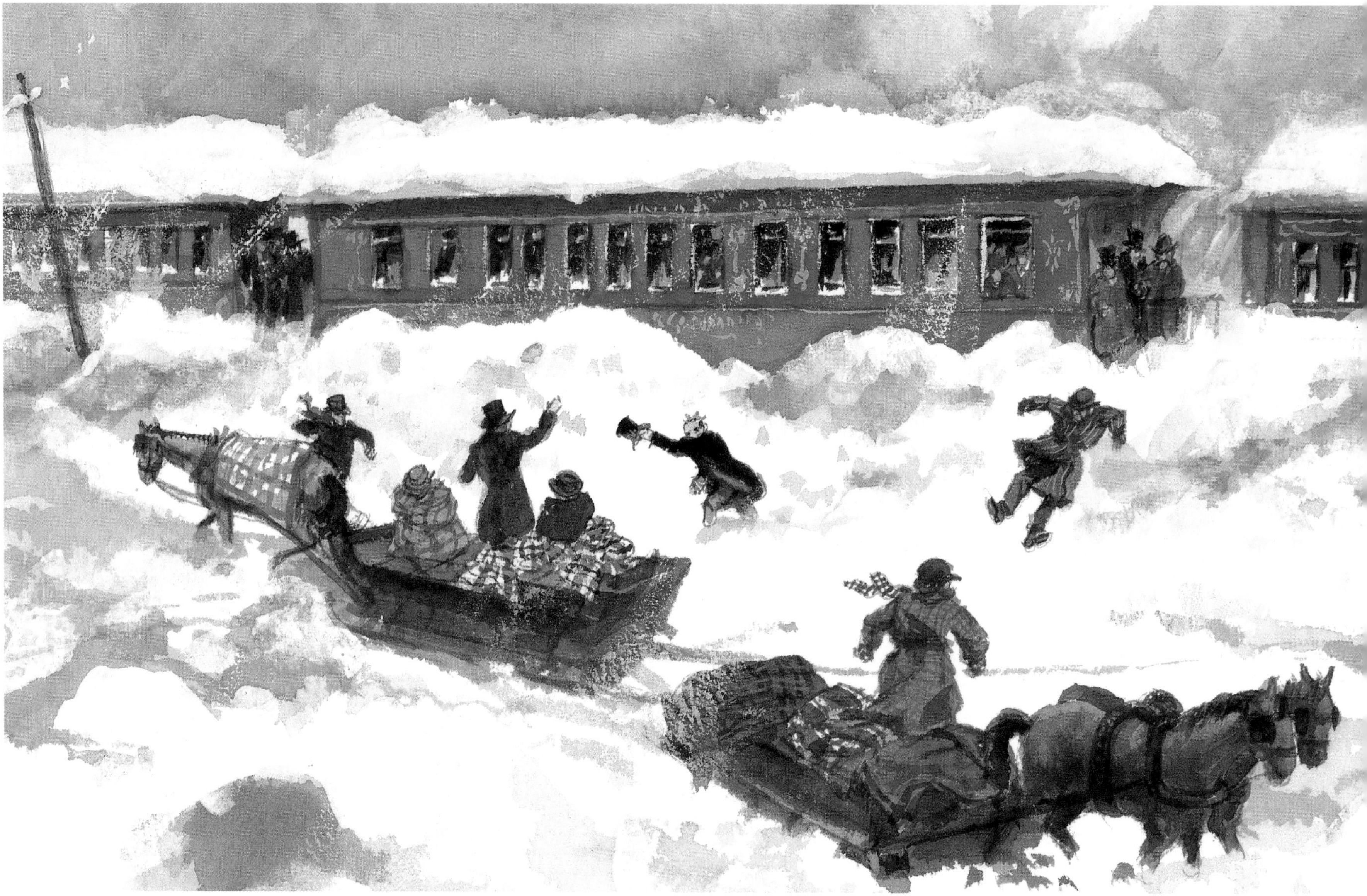

They heard bells jangling. A sleigh drew alongside the train. "All aboard for the Hotel and Saloon Rest-in-Peace, Rock Springs," the driver hollered.

Another sleigh arrived. "Jump on for the Dusty Dude Hotel and Dance Hall, Green River. Wait for the train in the lap of luxury!"

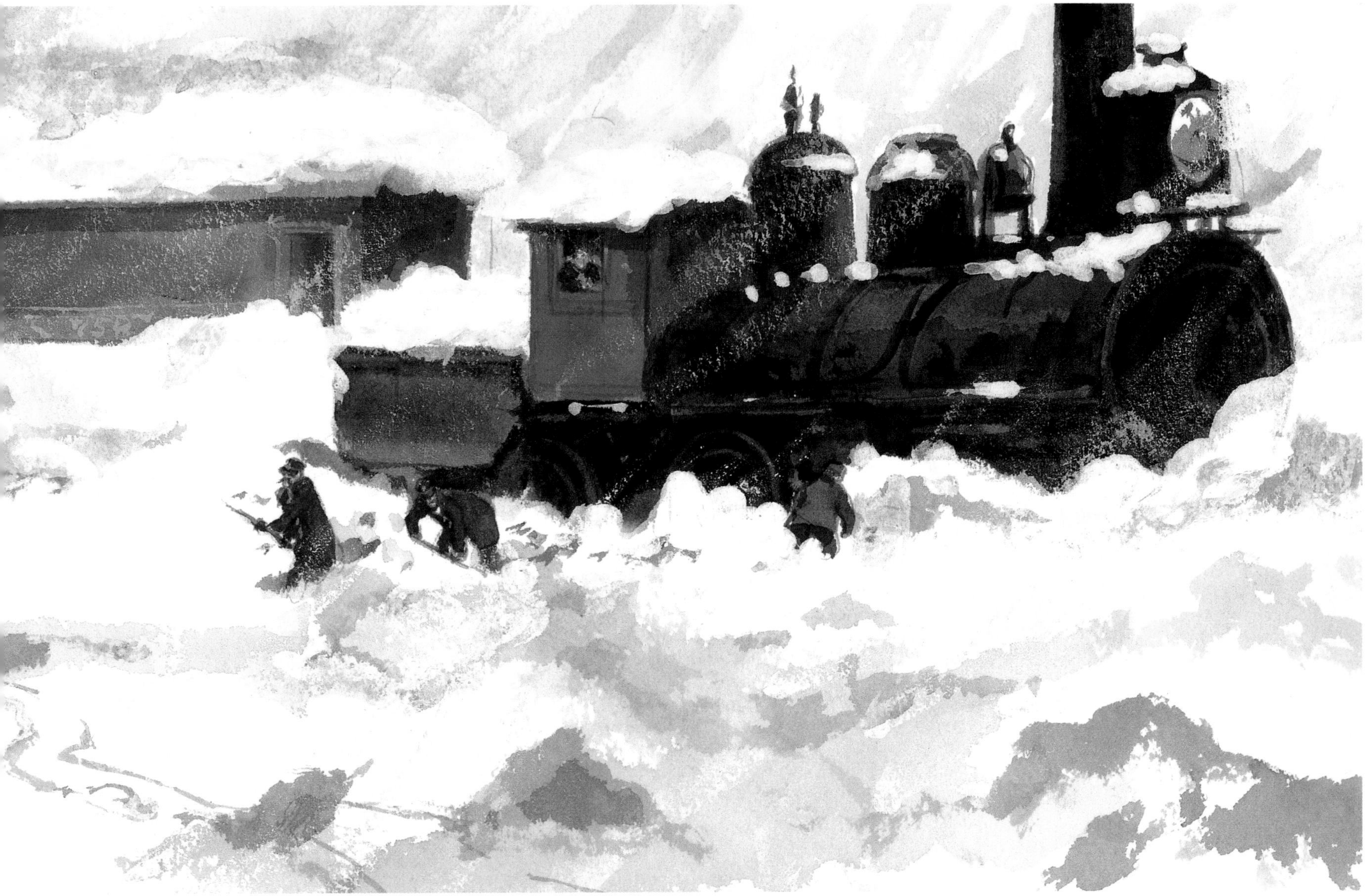

"Mama, let's go to a hotel," Clara cried. People were streaming from the train to board the sleighs.

"Goodness, no," Mama said. "They'll have bedbugs and all sorts of riffraff."

"You've got to go, ma'am, or freeze to death," Mr. Jones said gently.

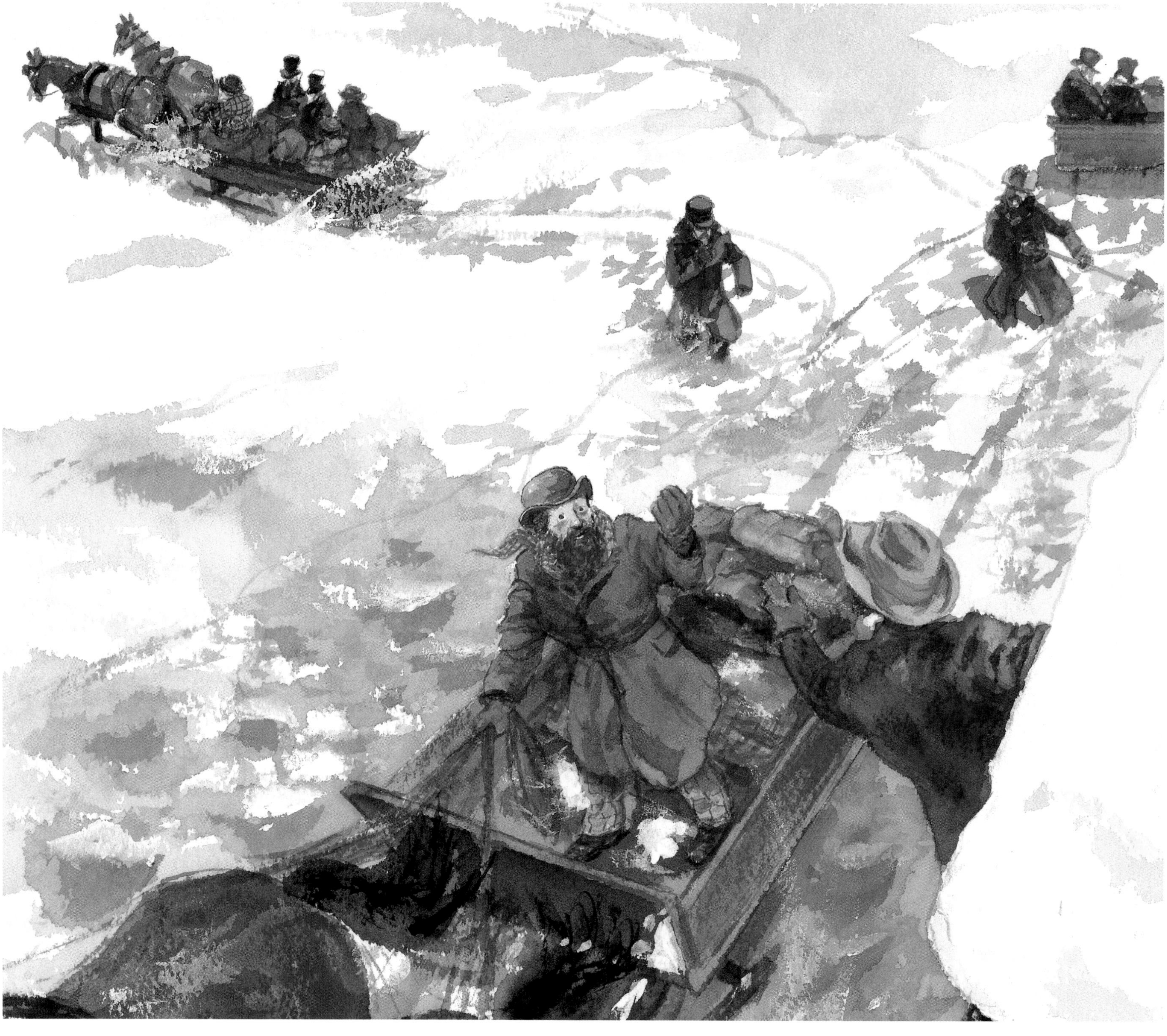

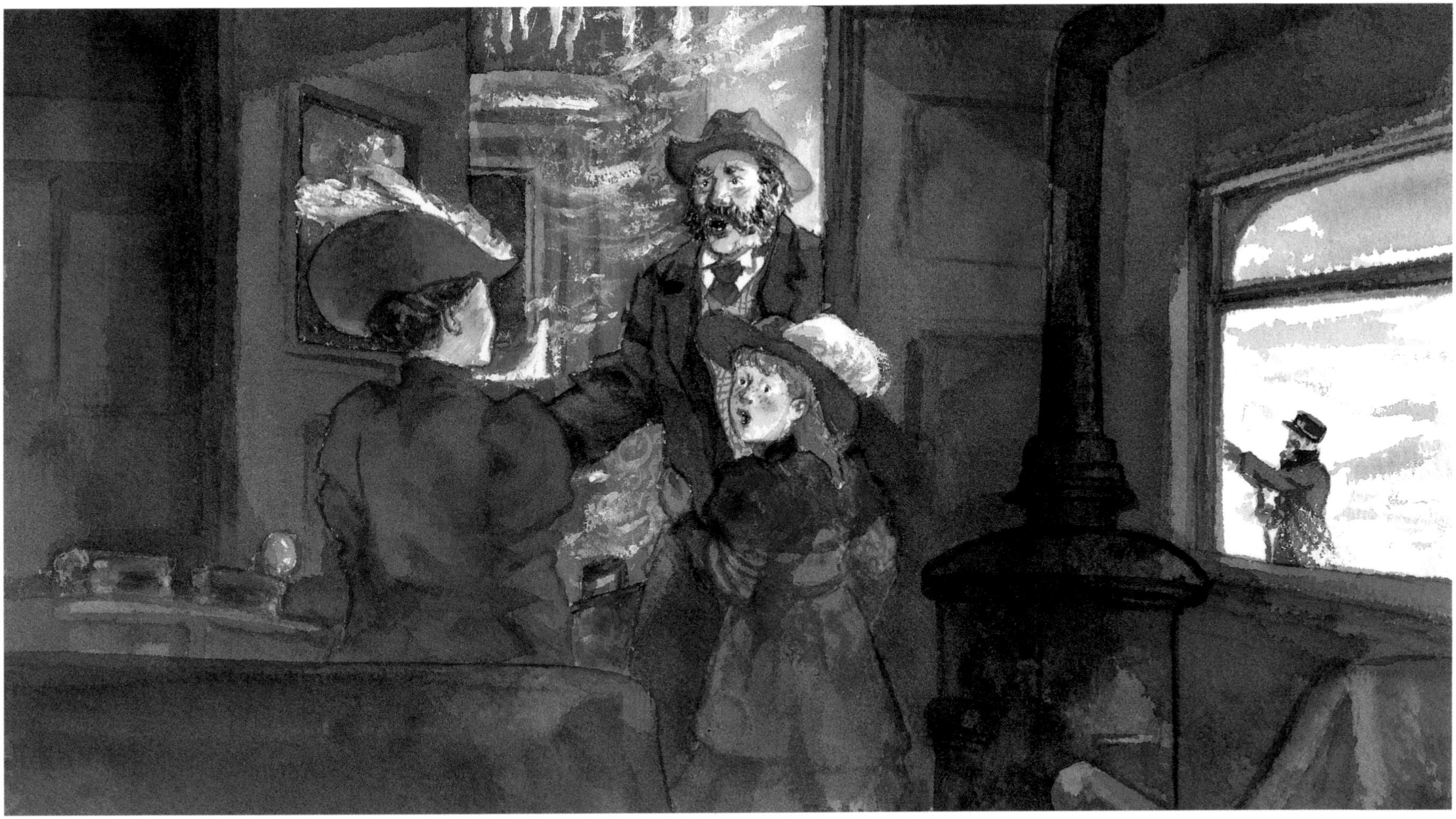

A smaller sled had arrived. “Where do you want to go?” the driver hollered.

Mr. Jones shouted, “I’ll give you fifty dollars to take me to Brown’s Hole.”

“Git in!” cried the driver exuberantly. Mr. Jones turned to Mama.

“Come with me to Brown’s Hole, ma’am. It’s just over the border in Utah. We’re respectable ranchers down there. You’ll get a real Thanksgiving dinner while you wait for the train to move. It’ll be a few days before they can dig it out.”

Mama sighed. “We haven’t any choice. Thank you, Mr. Jones.”

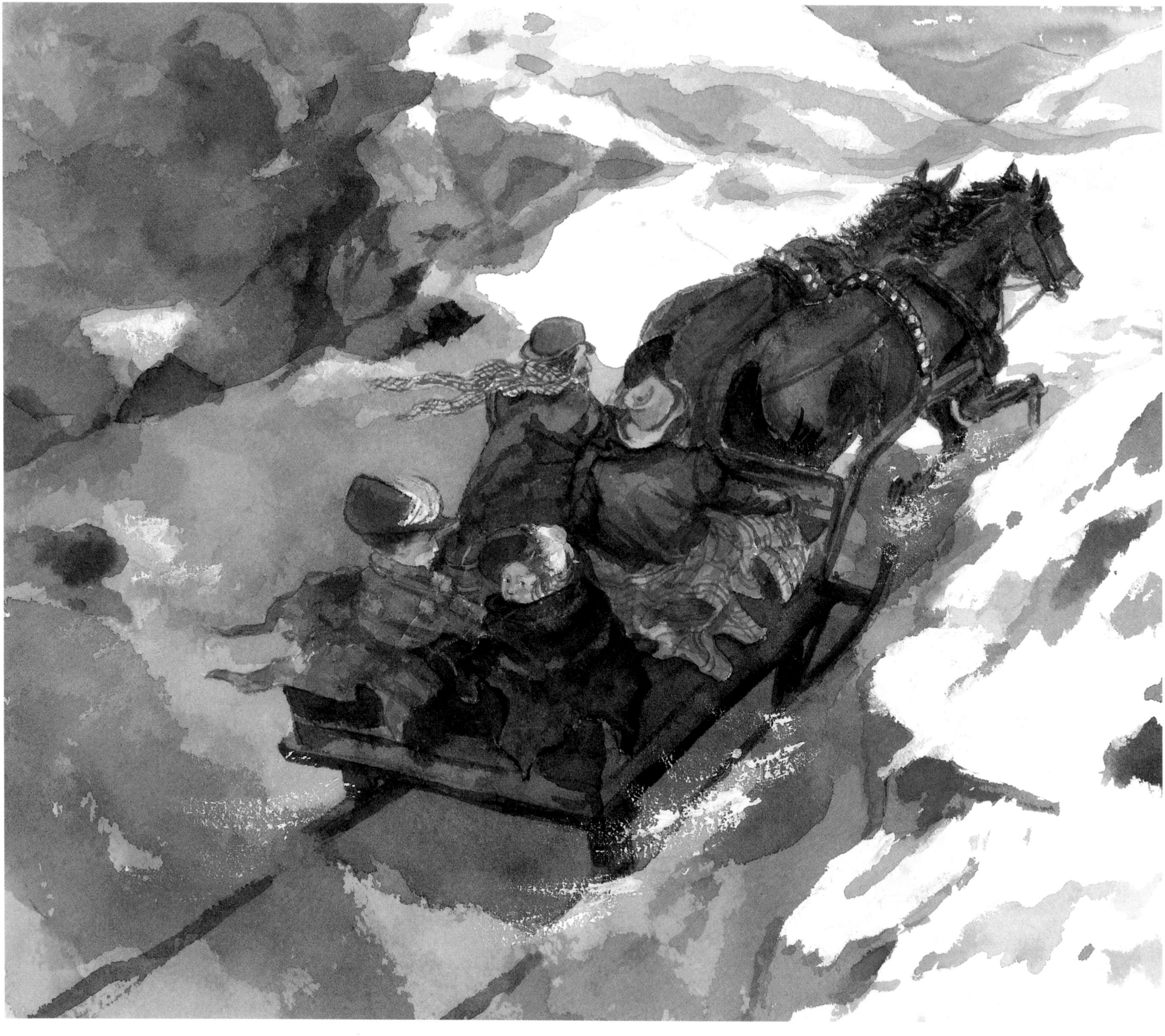

It seemed they had traveled for hours when Mama called out, "How much longer will it take us to get to Brown's Hole, Mr. Jones?"

His voice trailed back to them. "A day and a half, I reckon. Just in time for our dinner."

Mama turned white with shock. Even to Clara, snow stinging her cheeks, it seemed Mr. Jones had played a terrible joke on them. But there was no way out of it now.

The runners hissed and scraped. After darkness fell, they found themselves in a cabin, where a gruff woman put them to bed. At dawn she gave them coffee and biscuits before they set off again.

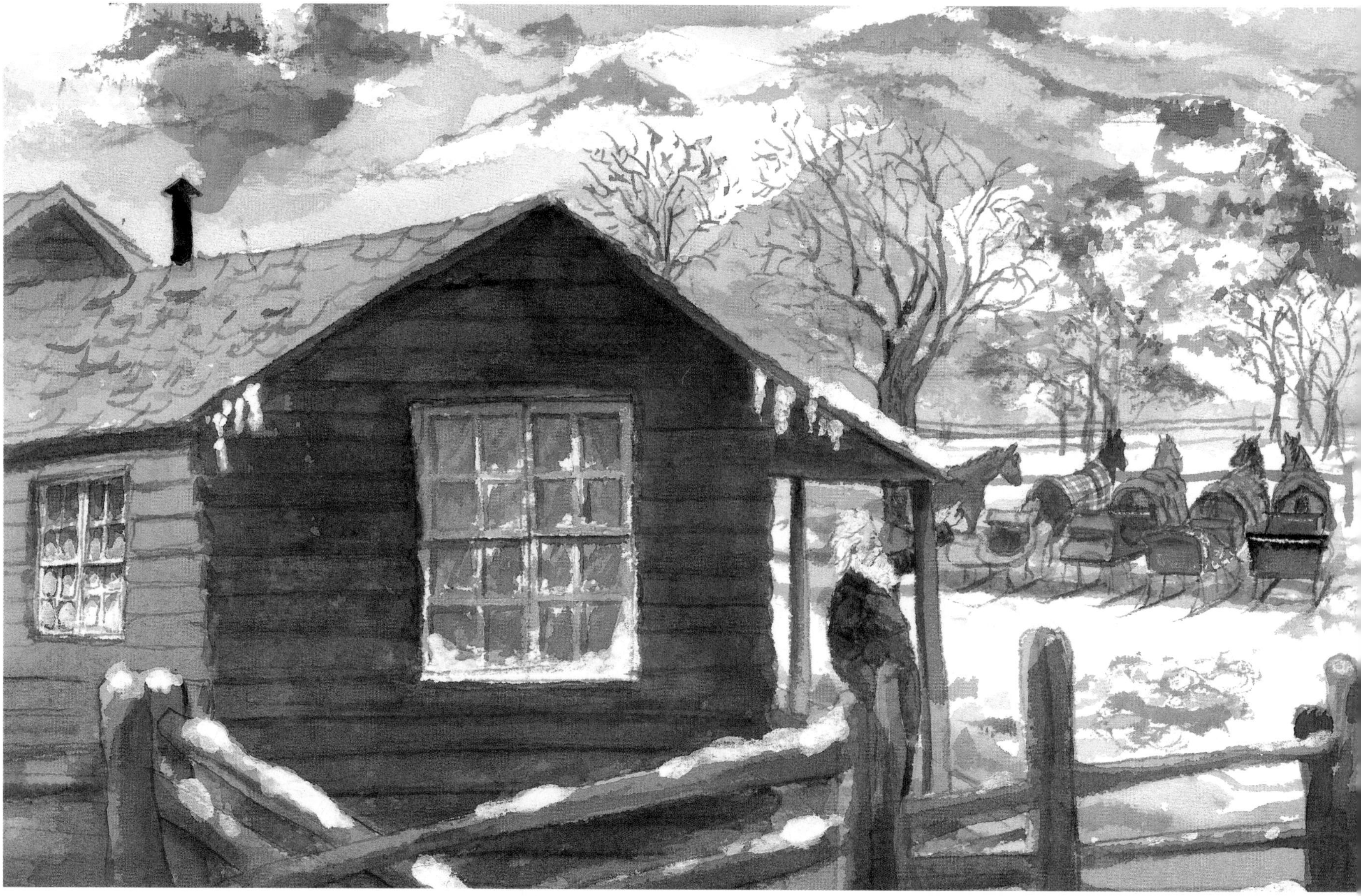

At last they emerged from a canyon into a wide valley. The sun warmed them as they pulled up to the log house where the dinner would be held.

A man bounded out. "Welcome to Brown's Hole, wayfarers," he said in a thick Scots brogue. "I'm John Jarvie. Howdy, Jones, didn't think you'd make it."

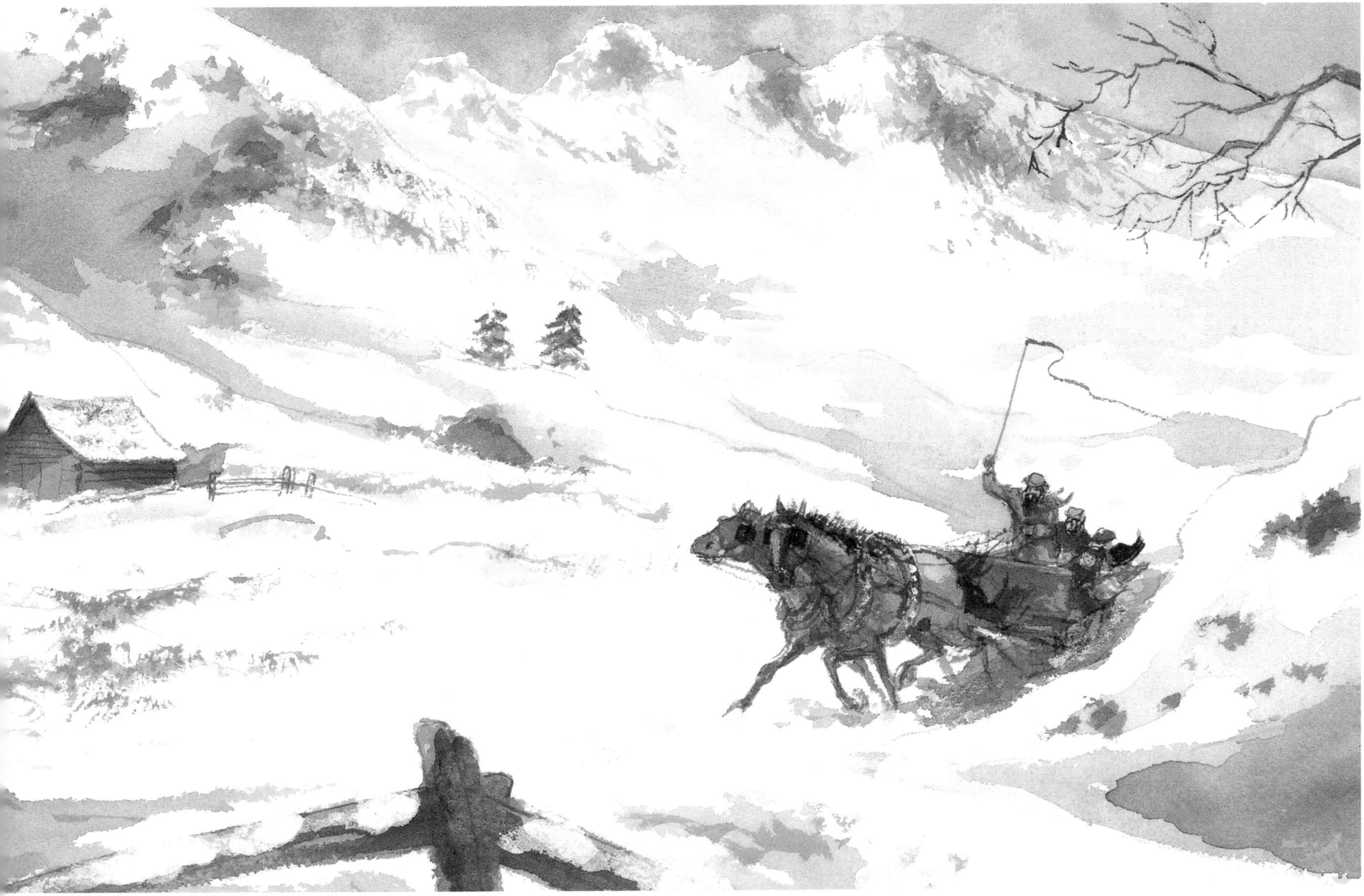

“We were all snowbound on the train,” Mr. Jones said. He introduced Mama and Clara to Jarvie, the local storekeeper.

“You’re brave pilgrims,” Jarvie said to Mama. “And you’re just in time. Some of our old cowhands are giving a banquet today for the residents of Brown’s Hole.”

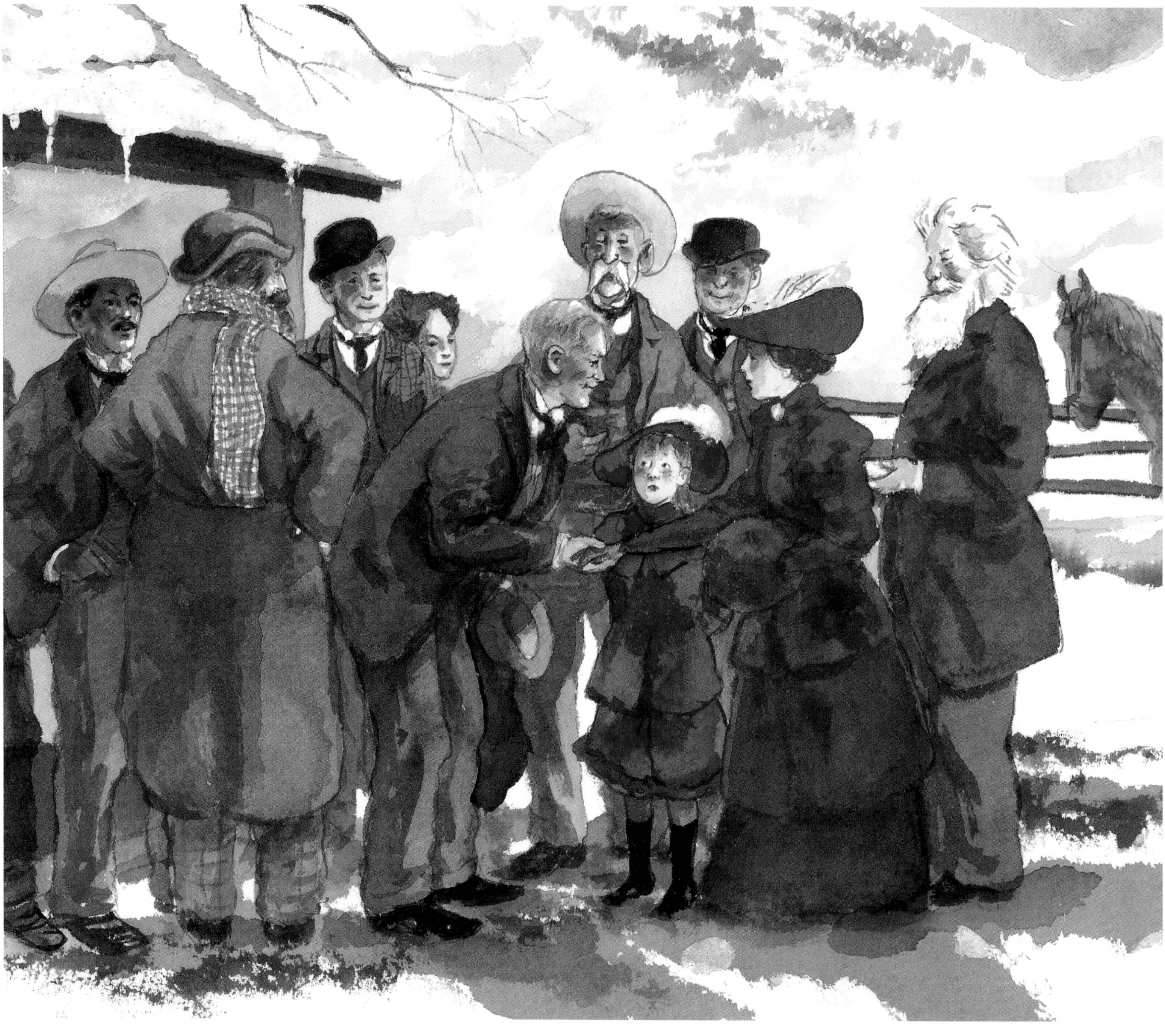

People streamed from the house to see who had come. "Let me introduce our hosts," said Jarvie. "Ladies, meet Bill, Les, Elza, Isom, ah, Bob, and Harry." Clara was startled, sure she had seen one of the men somewhere before.

Bob bowed low and kissed Mama's hand. "That brooch is most becoming, ma'am," he said.

"Such refined manners!" Mama whispered to Clara. "He looks familiar, doesn't he? I can't imagine where we could have met him."

A woman in a silk dress swished up to them. "I'm Ann Bassett. I'm famished and I reckon you are too!" she said, opening the door. Inside were long tables set with gleaming china, silver, and crystal.

"My!" Mama exclaimed.

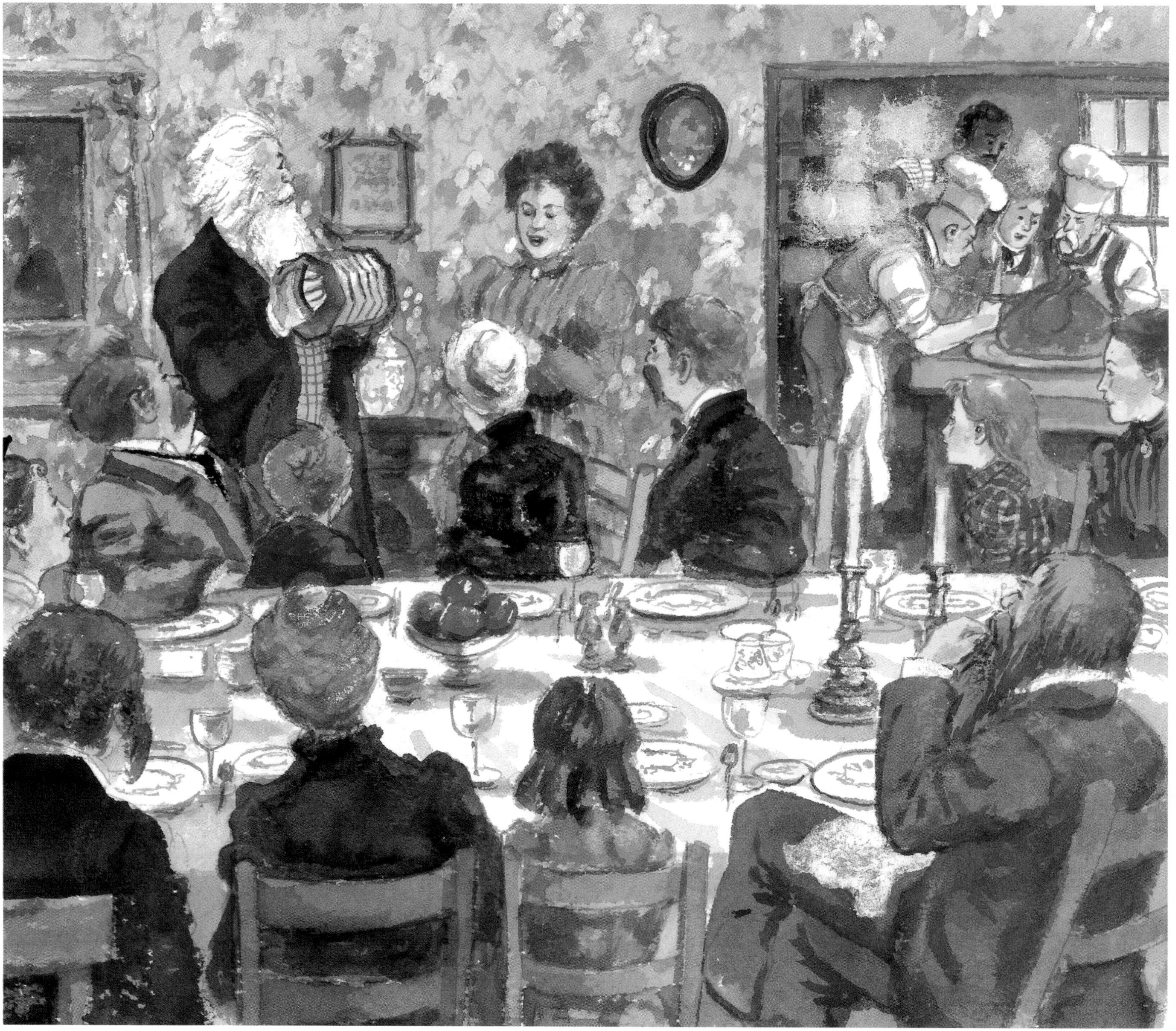

While Elza passed the relish tray, John Jarvie took up an accordion. He played and the guests sang "Then You'll Remember Me." Ann Bassett delivered a short talk on the meaning of Thanksgiving. "I coached her myself," Jarvie said.

Bob and the other hosts retired to the kitchen and could be seen scooping food onto platters. Their voices carried into the room. "You carve, Les!" "Naw, let Elza." "Elza's all thumbs!" "Well, do I start at the neck or the tail?"

Jarvie tapped his glass. "Let us give thanks for our beloved Brown's Hole, for this magnificent feast, and for America, land of the free!" he declared. "Hear, hear!" everyone called. Mr. Jones winked at Clara from across the table. She felt as if he had led them into a dream, strange and familiar at the same time.

Clara ate everything: oysters, cran-
berries, turkey with chestnut stuffing,
mashed potatoes with giblet gravy,
sweet potatoes, cabbage, beets, beans,
creamed peas, celery, pickled walnuts
and sweet pickles, olives, fresh tomatoes
on crisp lettuce, hot rolls and sweet
butter, cheese, pumpkin pie, plum
pudding, mints, and salted nuts.
It was the biggest—and best—meal
she'd ever had.

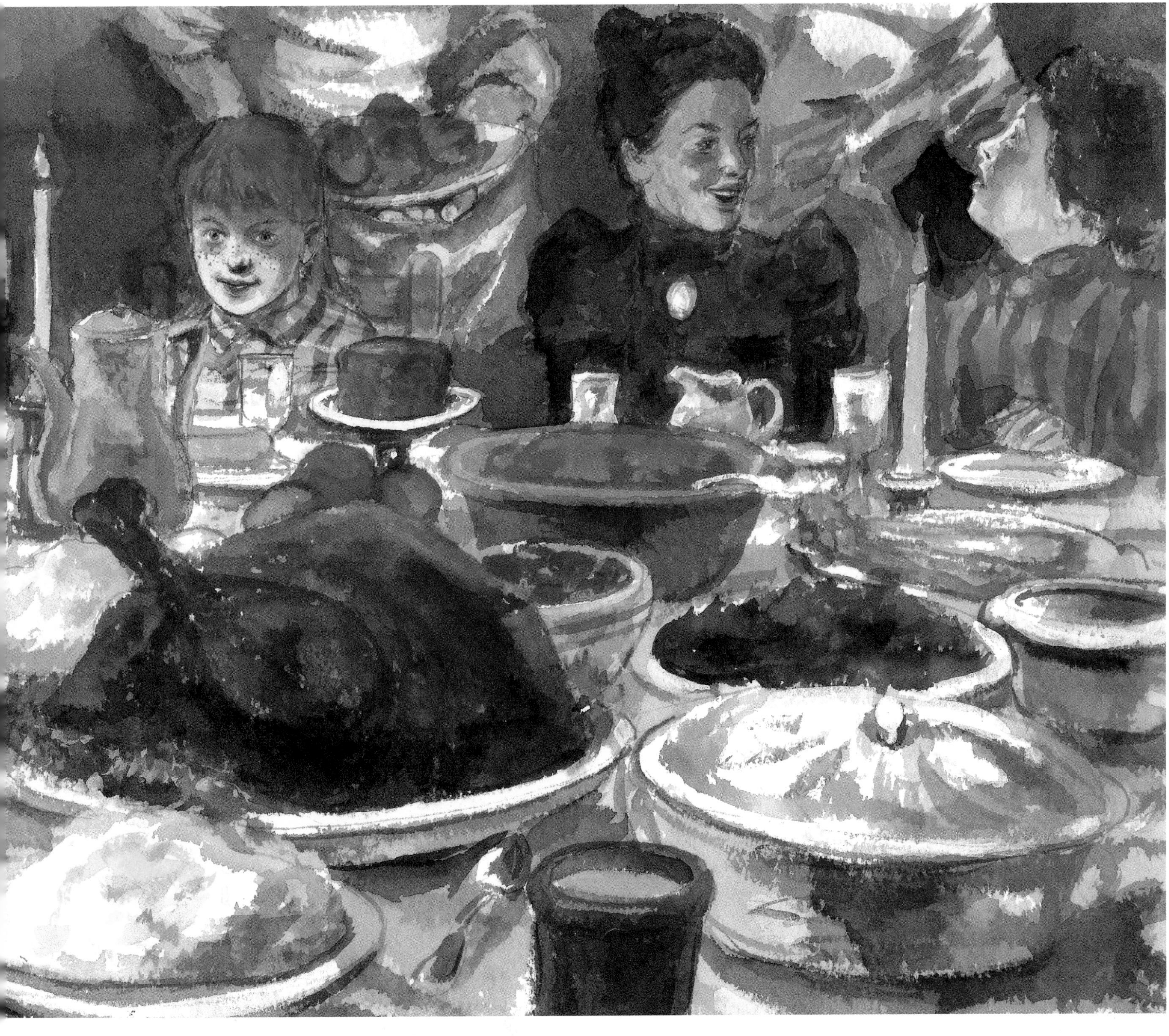

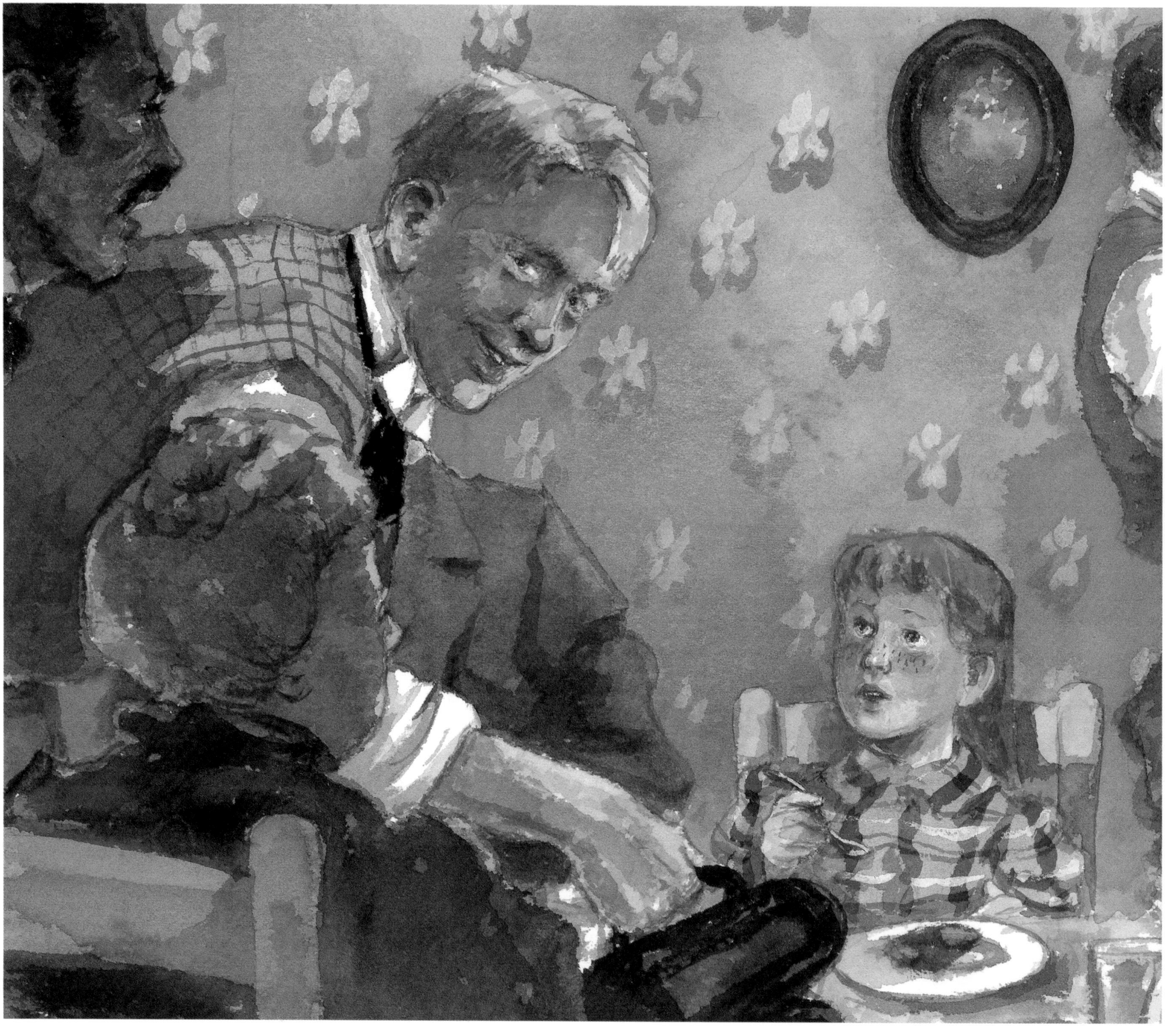

Bob bustled about, offering second helpings and thirds and even fourths. But when he came out with coffee, Isom yelled, "Ain't you never served a formal meal before? You properly pour from the right!"

"Well, you know how sorry my aim is, Isom," Bob answered. "The important thing is to hit the cup!"

"Etiquette can put fear into the bravest man's heart," said Miss Bassett. Mama laughed with the rest, but Clara, staring at Bob, heard a sudden echo: "He ain't afraid of the law or anything else."

That face on the poster . . . Robert LeRoy Parker! *Bob was Butch Cassidy!* And his friends—they must be outlaws too!

She glanced at Mama, who seemed to have forgotten all her worries. Clara must keep her from finding out they'd been led to a den of thieves. Poor Mama! She'd faint dead away if she knew.

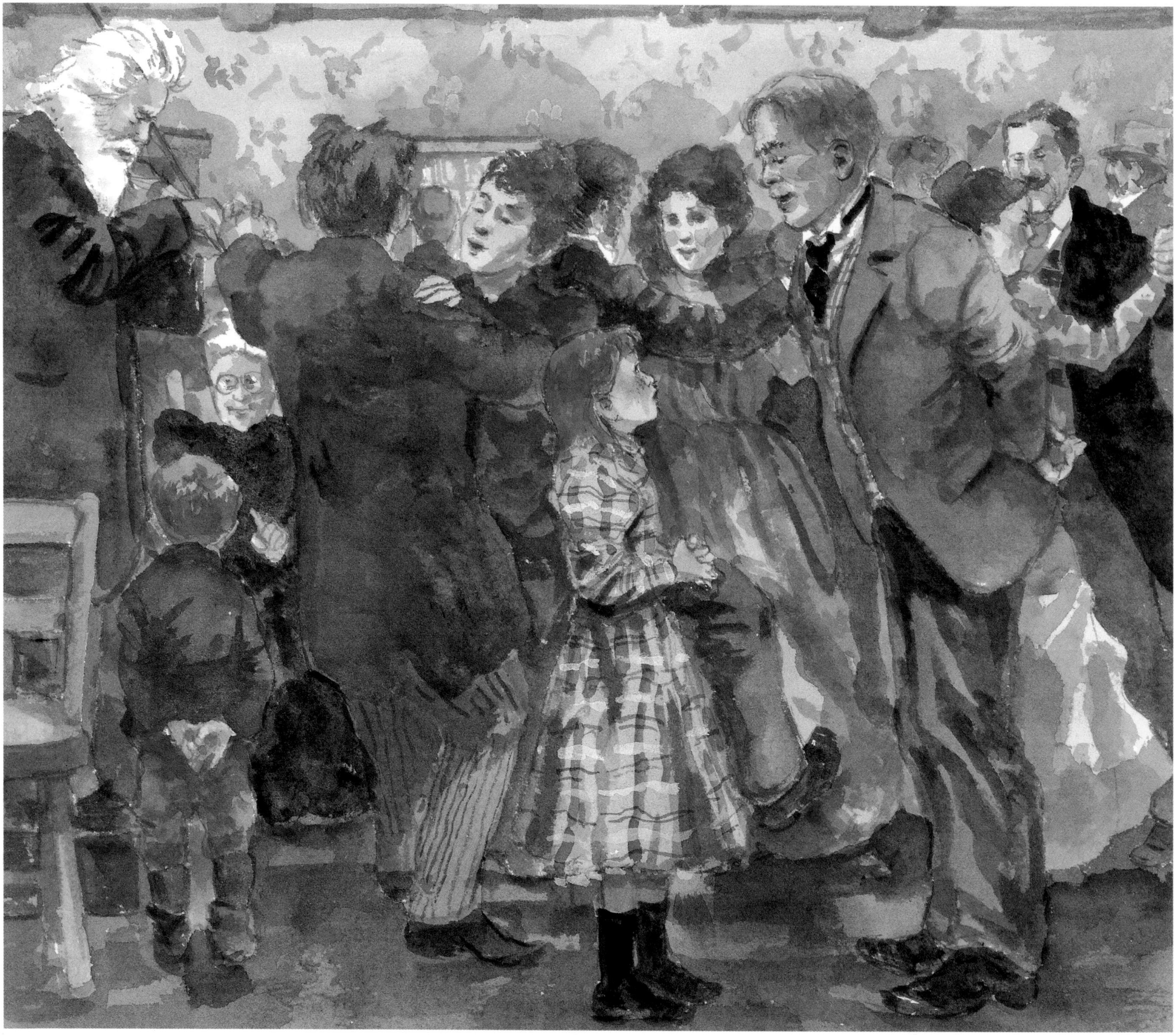

John Jarvie got out his fiddle and struck up "Turkey in the Straw." People danced. Clara watched to see who Bob—Butch—would choose for a partner. He came straight for her!

He bowed. "May I have this dance?" he asked.

Clara stared at him. His blue eyes twinkled. She had to be brave for Mama's sake. "Mr. Cassidy . . . are you going to rob our train?" she blurted.

Butch roared with laughter. "I saw right away that you were sharp," he said. "How did you know who I was?"

"I saw your picture on a poster," Clara said.

"Well, a poster don't tell the whole story of a man," Butch said. "We've all worked as cowhands here. These people have been good to us. And we're just saying thanks today." He winked. "We won't rob your train. I wouldn't want to scare your mama after she's had such a nice time."

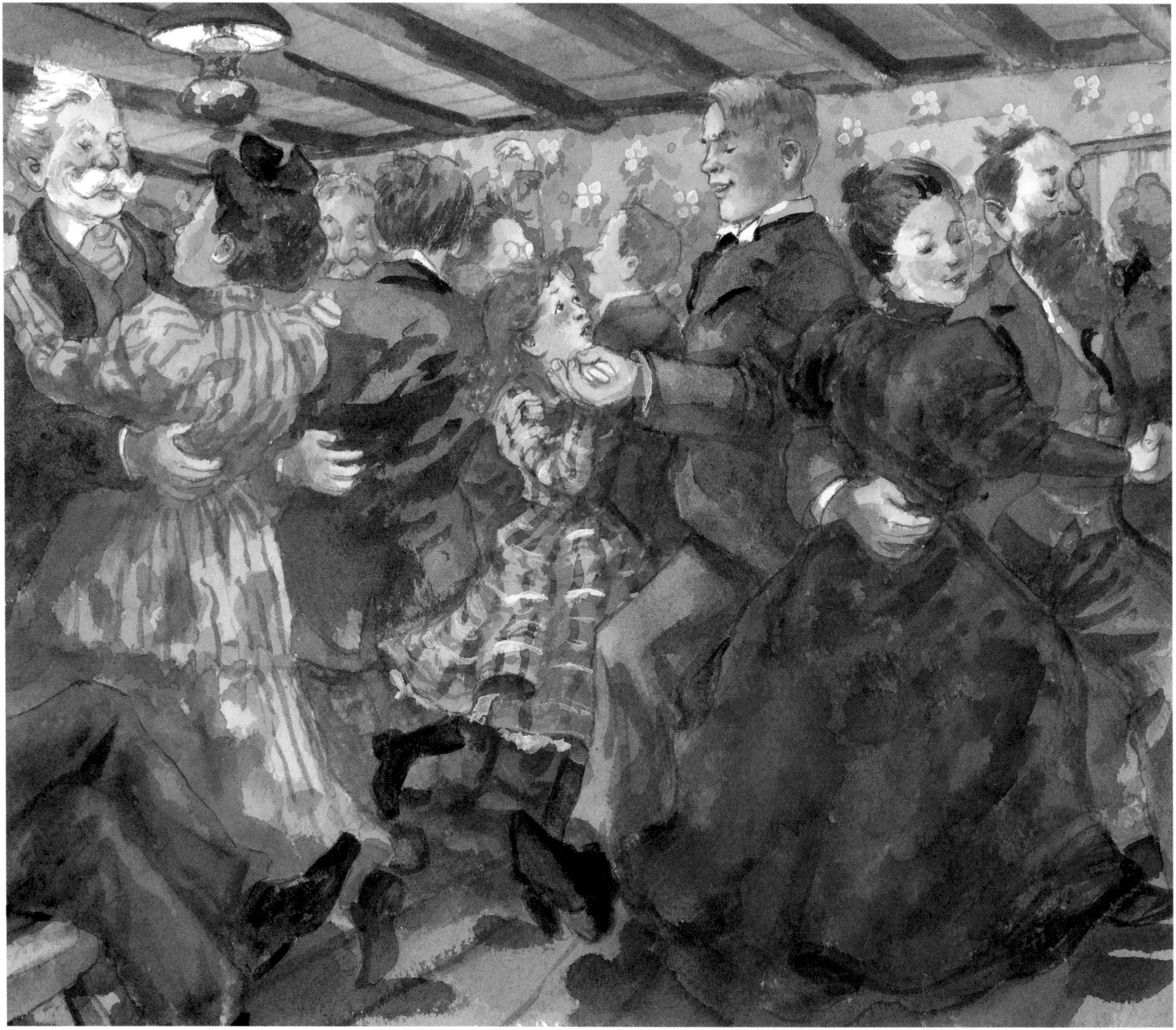

They danced a polka, whirling around the room until Clara was dizzy.

The dancing lasted all night. At the end of the party, Butch Cassidy took Clara's hand and closed it around a brand-new silver dollar. "Take this to remember the great Thanksgiving banquet at Brown's Hole," he said.

The dollar was warm in her fist. She wondered how he'd gotten it. "Thank you," she said. "I'll never spend it."

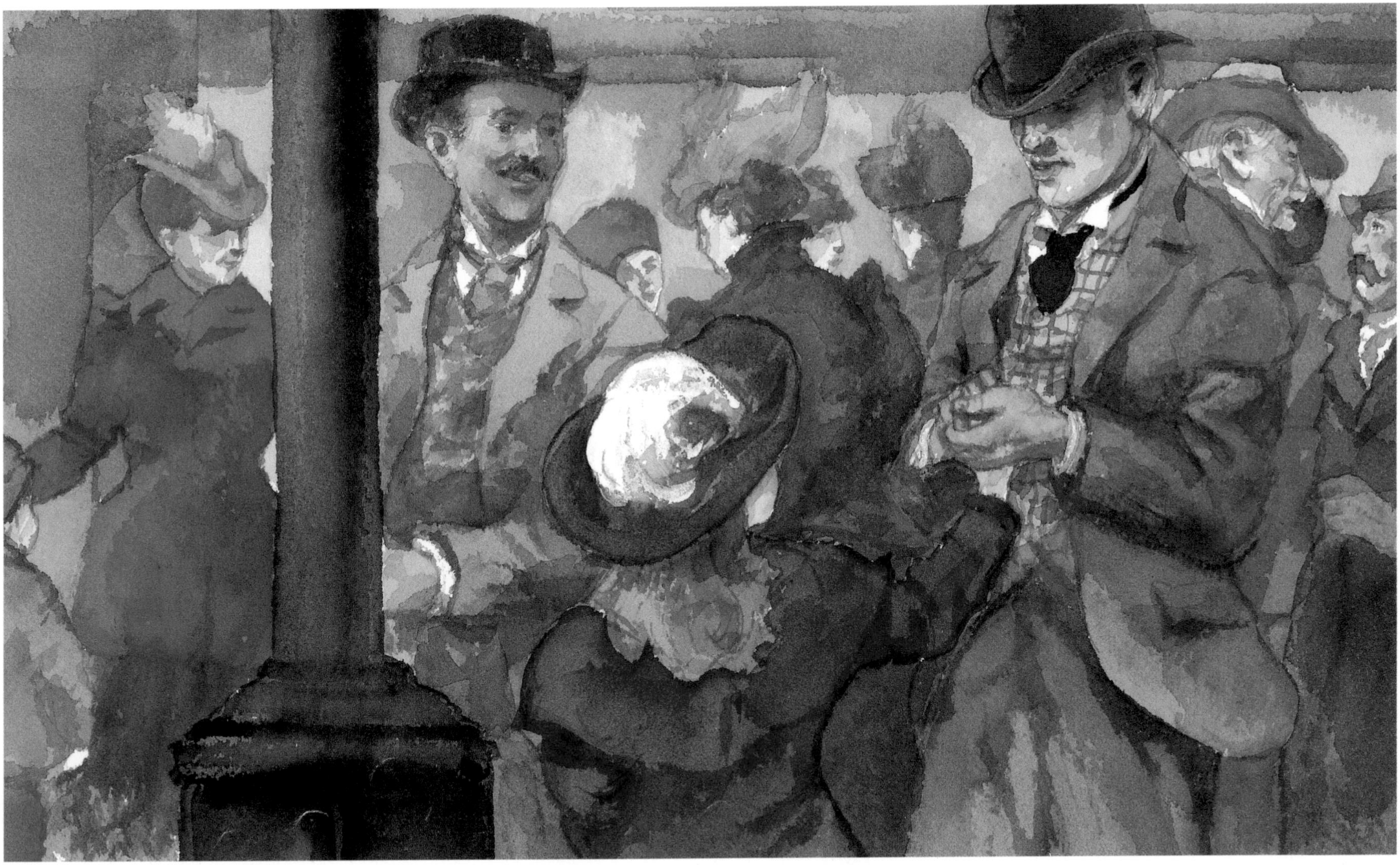

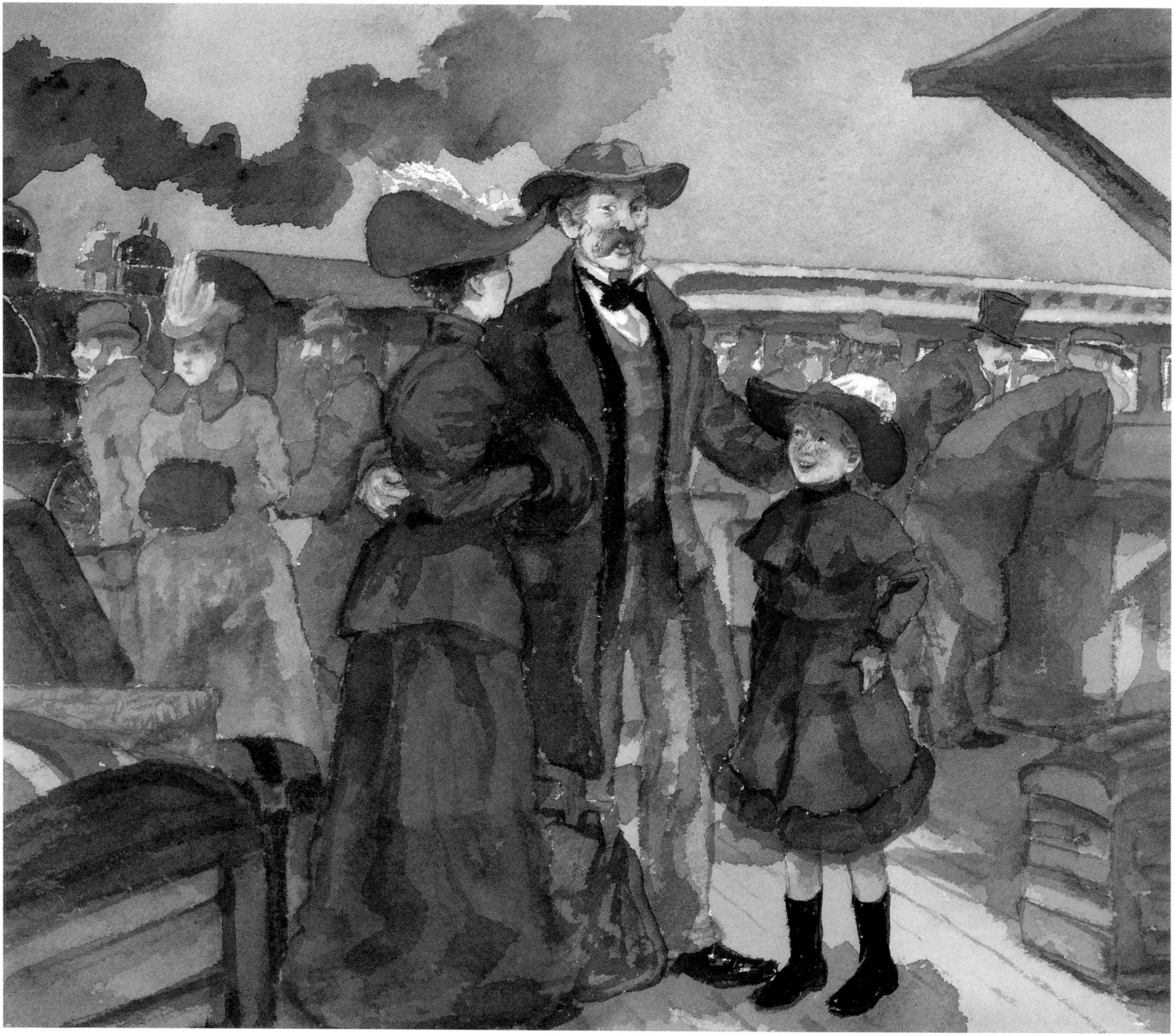

Clara and Mama stayed with John Jarvie's family. Two days later a messenger arrived with word that the track had been cleared. Jarvie's mail sled took them back to the train.

 When they finally saw Papa, they poured out the story of their unexpected Thanksgiving feast. "Everyone made us so welcome!" Mama told him.

"I'm sure they did," Papa said. "People are like that out here. Well, I missed Thanksgiving, but I'm mighty thankful we're safely together."

"So am I," Clara said. Should she tell Papa they'd been guests of Butch Cassidy and a gang of outlaws? she wondered.

I'll tell him when we get to California, she decided. And I'll keep my eyes peeled the rest of the way west. Out here, you never know what will happen next!

AUTHOR'S NOTE

By 1896 the United States was on the verge of the golden age of railroads. Trains with opulent Pullman, dining, and parlor cars crossed the country, though most people could only afford to travel in the coach cars. While much faster than any other means of transportation, rail travel still wasn't safe. Air brakes were new. Time zones had been instituted a decade earlier, making synchronization possible and avoiding head-on collisions. But owners charged whatever the traffic would bear and put safety far behind profits.

Snow was a problem for six or seven months of the year on the prairie. Passengers could perish in a blizzard. "Snowbucker" plows rammed into drifts at sixty-five miles per hour. Some disappeared into the drifts and stalled, trapping the crews. In the 1880's a Canadian invented the rotary plow, which chewed up the snow and threw it aside at a stately pace of six miles per hour. Clara's train might have had to wait quite a while for one to be available.

Railroads had speeded up the settling of the country, helping to create vast wealth. But the wealth went mostly to the owners, who used cutthroat methods and bribes to create monopolies and eliminate competition. Since corruption, exploitation, and greed were the earmarks of the railroad "robber barons," it isn't surprising that an outlaw like Butch Cassidy, with a reputation for charitable acts as well as for robbing trains, was popular.

Butch and his gang had been youthful cowhands in Brown's Hole (or Brown's Park, as some preferred to call it). For several years before and after the turn of the century, this ranching community, with only a few trappings of civilization, was a favorite place for outlaws to hide out. "Queen Ann" Bassett, a well-bred woman who could rope a calf or shoot a target as well as any man, was one of its residents; Scottish storekeeper John Jarvie was another. The ranchers tolerated the presence of the outlaws, who really did throw a Thanksgiving banquet for their friends at Brown's Hole. The hosts for the banquet were Butch Cassidy; Harry Longabaugh, the Sundance Kid; Billie Bender and Les Megs, leaders of the Bender Gang; Elza Lay and Isom Dart. Ann Bassett would recall the banquet years later, so that it could be re-created for women's clubs in Maybell, Colorado, and this fictional story of two unexpected guests at the dinner is based on her account. Bassett recollected the date as "around 1895"—though since Butch Cassidy was in jail during that time, a date of 1896 seemed more accurate for my story.

Ironically, John Jarvie would die at the hands of two petty thieves after the turn of the century. His store is maintained today by the Utah Bureau of Land Management and is open to visitors.